Ex

MW00882532

Cozy Mystery Series Book Fourteen

Hope Callaghan

hopecallaghan.com
Copyright © 2020
All rights reserved.

*****

Visit my website for new releases and special offers: hopecallaghan.com

Acknowledgements

Thank you to these wonderful ladies who help make my books shine - Peggy H., Cindi G., Jean P., Wanda D., Barbara W. and Renate P. for taking the time to preview *Exes and Woes,* for the extra sets of eyes and for catching all of my mistakes.

Thank you to Alix, my Savannah expert, for sharing your knowledge of this special place.

A special THANKS to my reader review team:

Alice, Alta, Amary, Amy, Becky, Brenda, Carolyn, Cassie, Charlene, Christine, Debbie, Denota, Devan, Diann, Grace, Helen, Jo-Ann, Jean M, Judith, Meg, Megan, Linda, Polina, Rebecca, Rita, Theresa, Valerie, Virginia and Vicki.

CONTENTS

Cast of Characters

Carlita Garlucci. The widow of a mafia "made" man, Carlita promised her husband on his deathbed to get their sons out of the "family" business, so she moves from New York to the historic city of Savannah, Georgia. But escaping the family isn't as easy as she hoped it would be, and trouble follows Carlita to her new home.

Mercedes Garlucci. Carlita's daughter and the first to move to Savannah with her mother. An aspiring writer, Mercedes has a knack for finding mysteries and adventure and dragging her mother along for the ride.

Vincent Garlucci, Jr. Carlita's oldest son and a younger version of his father, Vinnie, is deeply entrenched in the family business and not at all interested in leaving New Jersey for the Deep South.

Tony Garlucci. Carlita's middle son and the second to follow his mother to Savannah. Tony is protective of both his mother and his sister, which is a good thing since the female Garlucci's are always in some sort of predicament.

Paulie Garlucci. Carlita's youngest son. Mayor of the small town of Clifton Falls, New York, Paulie never joined the "family business," content to live his life with his wife and young children away from a life of crime. His wife, Gina, rules the family household with an iron fist.

Chapter 1

Carlita's eyes followed Luigi Baruzzo as he strolled to the other side of the pawn shop and approached the weapon's case where a customer stood perusing the goods. "How's it going with Luigi?" she whispered to her son, Tony, who was standing next to her.

"So-so." Tony shrugged. "He's a little rough around the edges."

"Rough around the edges as in how?"

"You'll see. Just watch."

Luigi Baruzzo, a former mafia bodyguard, had made the decision to retire from the "family" while assigned to guarding Carlita's daughter-in-law, Brittney, during a recent visit to Savannah. He had asked the Garlucci family if he could take up residence with them – renting Carlita's vacant first-floor efficiency apartment.

Her initial response was "no," but after discussing it with her children, Carlita had decided to let him move in – on a temporary basis and provided he promised to give up his life of crime.

The Garluccis were also helping him by hiring him to work part-time at Ravello's, Carlita's Italian restaurant, and Savannah Swag, the family-owned pawn shop.

She had asked her son about how Luigi was working out and grown concerned with his vague replies. Determined to find out for herself, Carlita decided to drop by the pawn shop during his shift.

"Hmmm." She grabbed a bottle of window cleaner, a handful of paper towels and made her way to the jewelry counter, adjacent to the gun case and Luigi.

She watched as he removed a pistol from the case and turned it over in his hand. "If you're plannin' on

2

usin' this piece to persuade someone to see things your way, this ain't gonna create a sufficient level of fear. You wanna be able to back up any situation with force."

He set the gun on the counter, lifted the lapel of his leather jacket and pulled out a semi-automatic. "This baby, here, the Beretta Nano, can neutralize just about anything." He trained it on the side of the wall and pretended to fire off a shot.

The potential customer's eyes grew wide as he stared at Luigi. "I...I plan to purchase it for home safety. We've had a couple of recent robberies in my neighborhood, and I want to keep my family safe."

Luigi lowered the weapon, running a light hand over the smooth metal. "Then, this might be a little overkill," he chuckled. "Get it? Overkill?"

"It looks like a solid piece. I...think I'm gonna think it over," the man stammered.

Luigi leaned an elbow on the counter and lowered his voice. "I might have a friend who can keep an eye on your neighborhood." He rubbed his thumb across his fingers. "He's reasonably priced and offers a one hundred percent satisfaction guarantee."

Carlita dropped the bottle of cleaner on the counter and hurried over. "I can handle this from here."

"No need. I was just leaving." The man stumbled backward, never taking his eyes off Luigi until he was a safe distance away. He pivoted and dashed out the door.

Luigi waited until he passed by the front window before turning to Carlita. "Hey, Mrs. G."

A heavy sigh escaped Carlita's lips as she wondered how many other potential customers Luigi had scared off. "Hello, Luigi. How's the apartment?"

"It's great." Luigi put his gun back and then returned the pawn shop's gun to the case. "It's nice and quiet. Almost too quiet. It's takin' me some time to adjust. There ain't much action around here."

"Which is a good thing, right?"

"Yeah. Right."

"I thought I would stop by to invite you to our family's Thanksgiving dinner at the restaurant."

"Sure. I would love to come."

"Good. I should get going." Carlita smiled as a customer walked in the door, and Luigi made a beeline for him.

She cast an anxious glance in his direction and joined her son, who was still standing in the back. "I'm not sure working at a pawn shop is Luigi's passion."

"No." Tony shook his head. "I'm puttin' out some feelers to see if anyone in the area is looking for security detail."

"Have you checked with Dernice?" Carlita asked. "As far as I know, Elvira is still gone. She might need an extra hand with the security company."

"I planned to stop by there but haven't had time."

"I'll ask her. I've been wondering if she's heard from Elvira." Carlita patted his arm, watching as Luigi lead the customer to the jewelry case. "He's trying. We have to give him credit for that."

She told her son good-bye and then exited the pawn shop, making her way to Ravello's where everything was running smoothly. In fact, all of her businesses were running smoothly. Ravello's was turning a tidy profit. The pawn shop was making money. Carlita's apartments were all occupied.

The restaurant had opened for the day, and there were already several diners inside. Carlita greeted a couple who were seated near the entrance on her way to the kitchen, where she checked inventory levels before returning to her apartment.

Mercedes' bedroom door was ajar, and Carlita found her daughter seated at her corner desk, squinting at her laptop.

"Knock. Knock."

"Hey, Ma." Mercedes swiveled around. "You get a chance to check on Luigi?"

"I did. I'm not sure he's a good fit for the pawn shop. He's scarin' potential customers off." Carlita told her how he pulled out his semi-automatic and trained the weapon on the wall. "I thought the guy was gonna hit the floor."

She pointed at the computer. "How's the new story going?" Her daughter had recently finished writing her mafia series and was working on a new one, this one set in Savannah and nearby Tybee Island.

"It's moving right along. Vinnie gave me a few pointers, but I'm thinking I need to make a trip to Tybee for research."

"Our Vinnie?"

"Yeah."

"I've been meaning to call and check on that new grandson of mine."

Brittney and Vinnie's first child, also named Vincent, had arrived on Halloween eve. As soon as they got the news, Carlita and Mercedes had hopped in the car and driven north to New Jersey to meet the newest Garlucci family member.

During their brief visit, Carlita saw firsthand exactly how deeply her son had become entrenched in the Castellini family business. Despite her misgivings about his choice of employment, Vinnie seemed to love the prestige of his job as the casino's manager.

He and Brittney had recently completed renovations on their spacious penthouse, located on the casino's top floor. Their new home was ultra-modern with high-end finishes, imported Italian marble floors throughout, not to mention every conceivable high-tech security feature.

Baby Vinnie was the spitting image of her son and deceased husband. The visit flew by, and Carlita was sad the morning they packed their bags to head home.

Vinnie promised he, along with his wife and new son, would make the trip to Savannah for Christmas, giving his mother something to look forward to.

"The baby is good," Mercedes said. "We did a facetime chat. He's so stinkin' cute."

"Christmas is too far away." Carlita's throat clogged as she thought about how much she missed her children and grandchildren.

"It's okay, Ma. They'll be here before you know it. Don't forget, Paulie and his family are comin' down too. We're gonna have a full house."

"It will be wonderful to have the family all together again." Carlita's cell phone chirped, and she shifted her gaze. It was a text from Pirate Pete, confirming their date for Saturday evening. She tightened her grip on the phone as she tapped out a reply.

"Who is that?"

"Pete. He's confirming our Saturday night date."

"Ma's got a date," Mercedes sing-songed.

"Shush." Carlita waved dismissively. "It's no big deal." The phone started to ring. It was Pete calling. "That's him now."

"I wanted to remind you that you'll need to bring a warm jacket and wear comfortable shoes."

"I will. You sure you can't give me a hint about where we're going?"

"And spoil my surprise? You'll find out soon enough." Pete changed the subject. "How's it going with your new tenant?"

"Okay." Carlita stepped out of her daughter's bedroom and wandered into the living room. "I'm not sure having Luigi work as a part-time pawn shop employee is a good fit for him or for us."

"I might have a job – a one-time security gig – coming up." Pete explained that a group of insurance salesmen were in town for a convention and had booked his pirate ship for an evening event. "They're a wild bunch. Last year, they rented out my restaurant and ended up damaging some furniture. They're paying good money, but I could use an extra hand keeping 'em in line."

"Luigi has an excellent track record at keeping people in line."

"If you have time, why don't you bring him by the pirate ship later?"

"That would be great," Carlita said. "I think a security job would be right up Luigi's alley." She thanked Pete and promised to run it by her tenant.

Carlita ended the call. Her eyes drifted to the balcony doors where she had an unobstructed view of the back of Elvira's apartment, reminding her she was curious and wanted to find out if Dernice had heard from her troublesome sister.

Carlita slid her phone in her pocket. She was halfway to the front door when Mercedes emerged from her room. "Hey, Ma. You heading out again?"

"I want to track down Dernice to see if she might be interested in hiring Luigi."

"I need a break. I'll go with you." Mercedes pulled the door shut behind them and followed her mother down the stairs.

"I'm also wondering if she's heard from Elvira."

Elvira, Carlita's former tenant, had recently become despondent. Despite their best attempts, Dernice and Carlita had been unable to pull her out of her funk. Without warning, she had left town.

The women rounded the corner, nearly colliding with a police officer who stood blocking EC Investigative Services' entrance.

Chapter 2

A red-faced Dernice was standing in front of the building, motioning wildly, as she spoke to one of the officers.

"Now what?" Carlita muttered under her breath as she and her daughter eased in behind them.

"This is a security company," Dernice snapped. "Of course, I keep the doors locked when no one is here. I also have surveillance cameras, which aren't catching anything."

"There's no sign of forced entry. My men and I searched the place. As far as we can tell, no crime has been committed."

"I'm telling you, someone is messing around here," Dernice insisted.

The officer shrugged helplessly. "There's nothing I can do other than put in a request for some extra patrols."

Dernice folded her arms, making a grunting sound as she watched the officers climb into the patrol car and drive off.

"What happened?" Carlita asked.

"This is the second time this week that I came back from a job and found the front door wide open. I know for a fact I locked it." Dernice explained that the first time it happened, she thought she'd been in a hurry and had forgotten to shut it, but now that it had happened a second time, she was sure someone had been inside.

"They didn't take anything?" Mercedes asked.

"Nope. That's the weird part. I don't get it." Dernice placed both hands on her hips.

"Maybe it was Elvira," Carlita suggested.

"I already thought about that. The surveillance cameras should've recorded her or whoever it was. Elvira must've gotten the things dirt cheap. They're nothing but hunks of junk."

"What about employees?" Mercedes shaded her eyes and studied the street. "Could it be an employee or ex-employee messing around?"

"I change the locks every time an employee is terminated or quits." Dernice turned to Carlita. "Speaking of Elvira, she needs to get her butt back here. I'm swamped with holiday jobs."

"As a matter of fact, that's one of the reasons I'm here. You met Luigi, the man from...up north, my new tenant."

"Yeah. Yeah. We've chatted a couple of times in the parking lot. He seems like a nice enough guy."

"Luigi has been helping us at the restaurant and the pawn shop, but I'm not sure either place is a good fit for him." Carlita clasped her hands. "I thought EC Security Services might want to consider hiring him. He has experience in security detail as a bodyguard for my daughter-in-law and her family."

Dernice brightened. "Hiring someone who has experience would be awesome." Her smile quickly faded. "Elvira mentioned family ties from up north. He's not gonna start shootin' people or shaking them down, is he?"

"I…" Carlita needed to choose her words carefully, yet be completely honest with Dernice. The last thing she wanted was to cause the woman additional grief. "All I can tell you is he's trying to stay on the right side of the law."

"Good enough for me. I might have a job for him by tomorrow. I could use it as a trial run to see how he works out before offering him full-time employment."

"That's a wise decision. I'll have him stop by later." Carlita changed the subject. "Any word from your sister?"

"I talk to her more now than when we were living under the same roof. Great." Dernice's eyes followed a mail delivery truck as it parked near the curb, and the driver got out.

The mailman joined them on the sidewalk, carrying a small stack of mail.

"Back again?" Dernice asked.

"I am. Are you going to sign for a certified letter today?"

"Maybe tomorrow. Unless you wanna give it to me without a signature." Dernice leaned forward. "Is it the same one from yesterday, from the same law firm?"

"It is. I can't give it to you until you sign."

"What happens if I don't sign?"

"After the third attempt, we return it to the sender."

"Hang on." Dernice ran into the building and came back, waving her phone. "Can I take a picture of it? I want to send it to my sister."

The mailman paused for a moment and then shrugged. "Sure. No law says you can't take a picture."

Dernice snapped a picture of the envelope. "Come back tomorrow, and maybe I'll take it."

"Tomorrow will be my final delivery attempt."

"Gotcha." Dernice took the rest of the mail from him.

Carlita waited until he returned to his delivery truck. "What's that all about?"

Dernice studied her phone. "Blickman and Faust, Attorneys at Law, Hilton Head, South Carolina. They're sending something to Elvira."

"Why don't you sign for it?" Mercedes asked.

"Elvira told me that under no circumstances should I sign for any mail, and then she wanted to know who it was from."

"Elvira is having some legal issues," Carlita said.

"Could be. Or maybe it has something to do with another piece of mail she got. Check it out." Dernice motioned Carlita and her daughter inside the office. She snatched an envelope off the desk and handed it to her.

Mercedes leaned over her mother's shoulder as Carlita removed the contents. "It's a Warranty Deed."

"Yep."

"Tybee Island," Mercedes said. "She bought property on Tybee?"

"Check out the grantee...the buyer."

Carlita lowered her gaze, her eyes skimming the first paragraph. "EC Investment Group. You started an investment group?"

"Not me. This is the first I've heard of it. Remember when I told you Elvira cleaned out one of the business accounts? Now I know where all of the money went."

"I'd forgotten about that until you just mentioned it." Carlita thought about the day Elvira disappeared and remembered Dernice telling her that she'd emptied one of the business accounts on her way out of town. "Why is she buying property on Tybee Island?"

"I think I know." Mercedes snapped her fingers. "I've been doing some research on Tybee Island for my upcoming book. An investment company is snatching up properties near the beach. They plan to build a large entertainment complex along with housing and vacation rentals."

Dernice's eyes narrowed. "No kidding. Before Elvira went MIA, she was spending a lot of time working security detail on Tybee. She wouldn't let anyone else handle the accounts, insisting on taking care of them herself."

"Why wouldn't she just tell you she was starting an investment company?" Carlita shook her head, confused.

"We're talking about Elvira here," Dernice said.

"Good point. So now what?"

"There's an address on the deed. I want to check out the property. But first, I gotta handle a small employee issue at one of the jobs."

"Maybe you shouldn't go alone, to Tybee, I mean." Carlita tapped her chin thoughtfully. "If you wait a couple of hours, I'll see if Luigi is free. We'll tag along while you check out the property. At the same time, you can talk to him about a job."

"That's a great idea." Dernice walked them to the door as they set an agreed-upon time to meet in the alley parking lot.

"We'll be there, or at least I'll be there and hopefully Luigi too."

Dernice's cell phone chimed, and she glanced at the screen. "I gotta take this call. I'll meet you out back later."

Carlita gave her a thumbs up, and she and Mercedes headed out. "What do you think?"

"About what?" Mercedes asked.

"About Luigi working with Dernice."

"No one is gonna know how Luigi is gonna do unless they give him a chance."

They returned home and found Luigi standing on the stoop. He lit a cigarette and watched as they approached. "Your neighbors are quiet these days. Not much action goin' on."

"Speaking of action and neighbors, Dernice is looking to hire experienced security people. Would you be interested in talking to her?"

"Sure. Yeah." Luigi took a deep drag off the cigarette and blew the smoke over their heads. "I appreciate you helpin' me out. I'm not sure if being a pawn shop employee is the right career move for me."

"I agree. You need to explore some other options."

"I'm headin' in." Mercedes slipped past her mother and returned inside.

Carlita waited until she was gone. "My friend, Pirate Pete, the one who sneaked you and Ricco through the tunnel, is hosting a private event on his pirate ship and needs some security help, as well."

"Pirate ship?" Luigi flicked his ashes on the ground. "Sounds interesting."

"I think it might be a good start for you. It's next weekend." Carlita changed the subject. "Have you finished working today?"

"Yeah."

"If you have time, we can head over to the pirate ship to talk to Pete."

"I got nothin' but time on my hands."

"I'll be right back." Carlita ran up the stairs. She sent a quick text to Pete to give him a heads up they were on the way.

While they walked, Carlita chatted about life in Savannah, asking if Luigi had met any of the locals or made any friends.

"As a matter of fact, one of the other tenants, Cool Bones, invited me to check out him and his band at the Thirsty Crow. I played a little saxophone back in the day, and he invited me to jam out with them."

Despite Luigi's compact and broad girth, he moved at a quick clip.

"Cool Bones is a great guy," Carlita said breathlessly as she struggled to keep up.

"Sorry, Mrs. G." Luigi slowed. "I'm used to havin' to hustle."

"In more ways than one, I'm sure."

They passed the Parrot House, Pete's restaurant, crossing the street to Morrell Park. The park was not only home to the Waving Girl statue, but it was also the docking area for The Flying Gunner, Pete's pirate ship.

They reached the dock and side-stepped a trio of employees who were hosing off the gangplank. The workers waved them through and waited for them to climb the gangway and board the ship.

Pete's office was on the main deck, on the opposite side of the ship. Carlita gave his office door a light rap. She eased the door open when she heard a muffled reply.

"Carlita." Pete pushed his chair back and made his way across the room. "That was fast."

"Thanks for seeing us on such short notice. I'm sure you remember Luigi," she said as the men shook hands. "I explained to him that you're hosting a private event and need some extra help."

Luigi jabbed his thumb at his chest. "If you're lookin' for security, I'm the guy for the job."

"Guy for the job. Watch your booty," Gunner squawked. "It's a big job."

Luigi's head shot up as he eyed the parrot in the corner cage. "Who's this character?"

"Character is right," Carlita chuckled. "This is Gunner, Pete's parrot, and the namesake for this pirate ship."

Gunner strolled along his perch. "Gunner, the pirate."

"Gunner," Luigi snorted. "Like guns – gunner?"

"Rat-a-tat-tat," Gunner sang. "Don't let anyone steal your booty."

"Ain't nobody stealing Luigi's booty." Luigi leaned in.

Gunner lunged forward, clamping onto the tip of Luigi's fedora as he plucked it from his head. It dangled from the bird's beak for a second before he lost his grip, and it fell to the floor.

"Hey." Luigi grabbed it. "Don't be messin' with my fedora."

"Mess with the fedora," Gunner repeated. "Gunner is a pirate."

"You gotta watch him," Pete warned. "Gunner can move fast when he sees something he likes."

"Gunner wants a fedora."

Luigi shot the bird a look of irritation as he tightened his grip on the hat. "A fedora frocked nuisance."

"Let's have a seat." Pete motioned for Carlita and Luigi to join him. "I'm not sure if Carlita explained my situation. I'm hosting a lively – and by lively, I mean rowdy group of insurance salesmen for a private event on board The Flying Gunner Sunday evening. I have a few employees who will be helping with the security but could use someone with your level of expertise."

Luigi puffed up his chest. "I can handle whatever you got, even a bunch of suits."

"Don't let their profession fool you. It's a wild party crowd." Pete threw out a generous sum for the evening assignment, and Luigi quickly accepted before the conversation shifted to the upcoming holiday.

Luigi, bored with the conversation, began drumming his fingers on the arm of the chair.

Carlita stood. "We should get going."

"Yeah. I gotta get outta here. This room is a little too cramped for my liking." Luigi made his way to the door.

"Luigi!" Gunner yelled. "My fedora!"

Carlita burst out laughing as she approached Gunner's cage. "Do you want Carlita to buy you a fedora?"

"Pretty lady," Gunner said. "Gunner's fedora."

"I'm gonna step outside to have a smoke." Luigi tromped out of the office.

Carlita started to follow, but Pete reached out to stop her. "Thanks for stopping by, lass," he said softly.

Carlita could feel a warm flush fill her body. "You're welcome. Thank you for giving Luigi a chance."

He looked as if he was going to say something else.

"What?"

"Nothing. Luigi seems like a good guy." Pete released his grip. "I best let you get going."

The couple joined Luigi, who was talking to the deckhands.

She turned to Pete. Their eyes met, his dark and unreadable. Her heart did a little flip, and she quickly looked away.

Luigi shifted his attention to them, unaware of the exchange. "Ready?"

"Yes." She gave Pete a shy smile. "Thanks again for offering Luigi a job."

"My pleasure."

Carlita could feel Pete's eyes on her as she and Luigi exited the docking area. They crested the incline and stepped onto the sidewalk.

"While we're pounding the pavement, I thought now might be a good time to talk about Dernice. She and I are taking a drive over to Tybee Island to check out a property her sister purchased."

"Tybee, huh?" Luigi shoved his hands in his jacket pockets. "Castellini was lookin' at an investment property over there. Some big bucks investors were plannin' on settin' up shop there, and he was lookin' to get in on the action. I'm up for a ride. I gotta get something cookin'. I can't keep depending on you for help."

"You're helping us, too," Carlita pointed out. "But I can see you want to make it on your own. I think you'll like working with Dernice."

Luigi was silent as they trudged back to Walton Square, passing by Annie Dowton's real estate office and the pawn shop. They circled the block and began making their way to Elvira's building.

Carlita had just stepped off the curb when she felt a tiny tremble, seconds before there was a loud explosion.

Chapter 3

There was a split second of eerie silence followed by the wail of an alarm.

"You stay here. I'm gonna check it out." Luigi rushed around the corner and out of sight.

The apartment building's back door flew open. Tony and Mercedes ran into the alley.

Tony was the first to spot his mother. "What's goin' on?"

"I don't know." Carlita pressed a trembling hand to her chest. "Luigi and I were heading next door to talk to Dernice when all of a sudden, there was this explosion."

"It sounded like a bomb going off," Mercedes said. "Are you okay?"

"I'm fine," Carlita sucked in a shaky breath. "It scared the daylights outta me. Luigi went to find out what happened."

Off in the distance, there was the faint echo of sirens. The sirens grew louder as a firetruck and two police cars raced past the alley entrance.

"Luigi ain't coming back. Let's go check it out." Tony led the way around the building. Several firefighters stood near Elvira's front entrance...or what was left of it. The bottom of the door was splintered, and the sidewalk was covered with shards of broken glass. "He's over there."

Out of the corner of her eye, Carlita caught a glimpse of an EC Security Services' van racing toward them. The van came to a screeching halt behind the fire truck. Dernice flew out of the vehicle, a look of panic on her face.

Carlita and her children sidestepped the firefighters and joined Luigi. "What happened?"

"From what I can tell, it was a gas explosion," Luigi said.

"Step back, folks." A firefighter waited for them to move away while a police officer began stringing caution tape along the sidewalk.

"I wonder what caused it." Carlita told the others what Dernice had said earlier, how she suspected someone had been inside the building, but nothing had been touched.

"Could be intentional. Maybe someone is targeting their investigative services company," Tony said.

"A disgruntled customer," Mercedes chimed in.

A Channel 11 News van arrived moments later. The crew exited the vehicle and began setting up their equipment. Brock Kensington, a local reporter, emerged. He swaggered onto the sidewalk and began smoothing his hair.

"Autumn can't stand that guy," Mercedes said.

Brock waited for the camera crew to give him the thumbs up. He approached one of the officers, turning so that they both faced the camera.

Kensington spent several moments interviewing him before approaching Dernice, who was standing next to a firefighter. She waved him off as she shook her head.

Not ready to give up, he shoved the microphone in her face.

Dernice glared at the reporter and pushed the microphone away. For a second, Carlita thought she was going to take a swing at him. The firefighter must've thought the same and stepped between them.

"He's telling the reporter to buzz off," Luigi said.

Kensington finally backed down. He leaned in and said something to his camera crew. They returned to their van and sat inside with the engine idling for a long time before slowly driving off.

The firefighters packed up their gear and hoses and drove away, leaving only the police officers and Dernice.

Tony consulted his watch. "As much as I'm dyin' to know what happened, I need to get back to work."

"This might take a while. I'll keep you posted," Carlita promised.

"I'm gonna take off too." Mercedes followed her brother, careful to steer clear of the taped off area as she made her way past the building.

"They're all leavin'." Carlita craned her neck, watching as one of the last officers on the scene jotted something on a notepad, and then tucked it into his front pocket.

Carlita and Luigi waited until he and his partner left before joining Dernice near the entrance.

"What happened?" Carlita asked.

"I was gonna take Elvira's rusty old propane tank to the store to swap it out for a new one. I left it by the door, so I wouldn't forget. It musta' had a leak, and something ignited it." Dernice's hands flew up. "The thing went off like a bomb and blew out my front door."

"Luigi and I heard the explosion. We were in the alley when it happened."

"Ten minutes earlier, and the tank would've gone off with me inside. I could've been blown to smithereens." Dernice began removing the police tape. "It blew the glass right out of the door."

Shards of glass crunched under Carlita's shoes as they cautiously followed Dernice inside. The smell of rotten eggs hung in the air. "Is it safe to be in here?"

"Yeah. The firefighters checked the air quality before they left. Remember how I called the cops earlier because I thought someone was messing around but didn't see anything on the surveillance cameras? I was wrong. The cameras did catch someone. Check this out." Dernice removed a silver laptop from the desk drawer, placed it on top and lifted the lid.

The trio watched as a dark, four-door sedan crept by. An arm shot out of the driver's side window.

"What are they doing?"

"I have no idea. Throwing something at the building?" Dernice shook her head.

"Can I see it again?" Luigi asked.

"Sure." Dernice played the clip again.

"It looks suspicious." Luigi shifted his feet. "When was this recorded?"

"This morning, around the same time I came back here and discovered the door was open."

"With no sign of forced entry," Luigi said.

"Nope."

Carlita pressed the tips of her fingers together. "Is there anything you can think of that may have happened recently, maybe a client's case that didn't go as planned?"

"It's against company policy to discuss client cases. Elvira would have a fit if she thought I was sharing confidential information."

"And where is Elvira?"

"Believe it or not, she's in St. Augustine." Dernice began rubbing her temples. "I can't take much more of this. She has plenty of time to run around, start new businesses and buy properties. Meanwhile, I'm stretched and stressed to the max."

"Which is why Luigi and I were on our way over in the first place," Carlita said. "You need help. Luigi has a security background."

"I do need help." Dernice popped out of the chair. "Before we get down to business, I want to show you what the firefighters found while they were checking the place."

Luigi and Carlita followed her through the apartment to a set of metal cabinets in the back. She opened a cabinet door and stepped aside. "I had no idea this was here."

Carlita's heart skipped a beat as she inched closer and peered inside. The base of the cabinet was missing. She could make out what appeared to be a door...a door that looked very familiar.

Chapter 4

"It's a trapdoor," Carlita said.

"One of the firefighters noticed a cutout on the floor. That's when we opened the cabinet and found the door. Mind lending a little muscle to pull the cabinet out of the way?" Dernice flexed her muscle and pointed at Luigi.

"Sure." Luigi stood at one end of the counter, Dernice at the other and Carlita in the middle.

On the count of three, they pulled. The cabinet made a cracking noise but refused to budge.

Dernice opened an end door and stuck her head inside. "There are a couple of screws keeping it in place." She ran out of the room, returned with a set of screwdrivers and made quick work of removing them.

The trio tried again, this time easily sliding the cabinet away from the wall.

Luigi and Carlita stepped off to the side as Dernice grasped the brass handle. "Here goes nothing." She pulled hard, but it refused to budge. "It's heavier than I thought."

"I'll open it."

Dernice moved out of the way, making room for Luigi. The door was no match for his strength. He easily lifted it and then leaned it against the wall.

A strong, musty smell wafted up.

Dernice cautiously peered over the edge. "It's a pit of darkness. Let me grab a flashlight." She fumbled inside a nearby cabinet, pulled out a flashlight and shined it into the opening. The beam of light illuminated a wooden ladder. There was a dirt floor at the bottom.

Carlita could've sworn something furry and black scurried by. "You gonna check it out?"

"I..." Dernice swept the flashlight along the perimeter. "Later. I need to find out what's going on in Tybee first."

"Are you ready to head over there?" Carlita asked.

"Yeah. If you have time, I'm ready to go."

*****

During the drive to Tybee, Dernice vented about her sister, her secretive attitude and the trouble she was causing. Carlita didn't interrupt, and honestly, she couldn't disagree with anything she said.

It took them longer to find Elvira's property than it did to drive there. Dernice eased into an empty parking spot in front. The buildings on both sides were boarded up. All three were in a similar, sad state of disrepair.

It struck Carlita as odd that only one of the vacant buildings sported a for-sale sign. It was stapled to a sheet of plywood covering the front.

Dernice consulted a scrap of paper she dug out of her pocket and rattled off the address. "This is it."

They exited the vehicle and gathered near the entrance.

Dernice tried the door. "It's locked. Good thing I brought these." She removed a small tool from the case she was carrying and inserted it into the doorknob's keyhole. With a couple of twists, the door swung open.

"I'll go first." Luigi placed a light hand on his jacket pocket as he eased past the women and entered the building.

Empty shelves lined the right-hand wall. To the left were several storage boxes.

Carlita studied the stack of boxes. "Caution. Flammable materials." Emblazoned on the side of the top box was a fire symbol.

Dernice flipped the flaps and pulled out a bottle of nail polish remover. "This place must've been a beauty salon or supply store." She set the remover back inside. "I wonder if Elvira has even seen this place."

"Didn't you say she was handling the area's security detail right before she took off?"

"She was, and now that I think about it, we were hired a few months back to keep an eye on a business that was planning to build a large development." Dernice told them the company was being targeted by locals who were protesting the company's project.

"So when Elvira found out what was going on, she must have decided to buy a property, hoping to turn around and sell it for big bucks." Carlita tapped her chin thoughtfully.

"That's what I'm thinking."

The trio finished their search near the building's rear exit.

"Hang on." Luigi ran a light hand over the doorjamb. "Someone tried to get in."

"You're right, and it looks like it was recently."

Luigi tested the door. "It still opens and shuts." He slid the bolt across the top. "This flimsy lock ain't gonna stop someone from gettin' in here, not that there's anything worth stealing."

"Great. This is just one more thing for me to worry about," Dernice said.

With a final sweep of the building's interior, they climbed back into the van for the return trip. They had gone about a mile when Carlita noticed Dernice kept glancing in the rearview mirror. "Is everything all right?"

"I dunno." Dernice stopped for a red light and looked back again.

"What's wrong?"

"I think we're being followed."

"We are?" Carlita peered into the passenger side mirror. A black car was close behind them.

Luigi unbuckled his seatbelt and shifted so he could see through the rear cargo door windows. "They're tailgating."

"A little too close for comfort," Dernice said.

The van reached the stretch of road connecting the island with the mainland.

Carlita's gaze never wavered as she watched the car behind them continue to tailgate. There was a sudden jolt, and she grabbed the dashboard to steady herself. "What was that?"

"They bumped the van." Luigi pulled his gun from his pocket. "They're gonna do it..."

Before he could finish his sentence, there was another jolt. Dernice fought to maintain control as the van started to swerve.

The second jolt sent Luigi off balance. He quickly regained it and climbed over the seat. "I wanna roll the windows down."

"They don't open. You can slide the sides open."

"That'll have to do." Luigi crawled to the back corner. "Hang on."

There was another jolt. The jolt forced the front tires of the van onto the soft gravel, pulling them off the road.

The black sedan swerved, straddling their lane and the oncoming traffic lane.

Carlita's heart raced as the vehicle pulled even with them. The passenger side window lowered, and a gun appeared.

"They're gonna shoot!" Dernice jerked the wheel, sending their vehicle into a semi-spin.

Pop. Pop. The rapid-fire echo of gunshots filled the van.

Chapter 5

As if in slow motion, the van veered back onto the road before coming to a screeching halt.

Through the front windshield, Carlita watched as the sedan roared off, turning into a small black dot before disappearing.

"You all right?" Luigi vaulted over the bench seat.

"We…I think we're fine," Dernice answered in a shaky voice. "They were shooting at us."

"They wish. I got off the first shots," Luigi bragged. "I nailed the passenger side mirror too."

"Maybe it was a distracted driver who accidentally bumped us." Dernice cautiously steered the van back onto the road.

"Three times and with a gun pointed out the window?" Luigi shook his head. "Not a chance."

During the remainder of the drive, Carlita kept her eyes peeled, half-expecting the vehicle to reappear and either shoot at them or force them off the road again. She let out a sigh of relief when Dernice turned onto their street.

"Hey, Luigi, you got time to fill out some paperwork?" Dernice asked.

"You still interested in hiring me?"

"I like your style. You know how to handle yourself under pressure, not to mention you saved me...saved us from taking a bullet. I admire that in a man."

"Then, you got yourself a new employee."

When they were back at EC Security Services' office, Dernice handed Luigi an application.

His eyes skimmed the front. He flipped it over. "I don't have much of a work history."

"It doesn't matter." Dernice waved dismissively. "I found out everything I need to know on the trip back here. The paperwork is a formality. You got my back, and that's what matters most. Besides, I know you worked security detail for a mafia boss in New York and New Jersey."

"Mrs. G. told you that?"

"Elvira ran a thorough background check on each of the guests at Tony and Shelby's wedding a few months ago when she offered the company's security services as their wedding gift."

"She did?" Carlita briefly closed her eyes. "Why am I not surprised?"

"She was curious." Dernice cleared her throat. "Your skills are unique, and you get the job done."

"Get the job done?"

"Not only did you protect us, but the boss, the family kingpin, is still alive...right?" Dernice asked.

"Alive and kickin'. I like you gettin' right to it and not beating around the bush. I think we're gonna work good together." It didn't take long for Luigi to fill out the application. He signed his name and handed it back. "When do I start?"

"How about right now? I'll pay you a flat fee to guard the building for the next several days. I'll even throw in three hots and a cot if you want."

"I appreciate the offer for a place to stay, but I'm pretty comfortable in my apartment."

"Suit yourself," Dernice shrugged.

"I'll be back in ten to start patrols." Luigi followed Carlita out of the building. He waited until they were a safe distance away before speaking. "How well do you know this lady and her crazy sister?"

"Unfortunately, a little too well." Carlita explained how Elvira had been a former tenant. "I ended up evicting her. The last straw was when she set her apartment on fire. Instead of me getting rid of her, she bought the building next door. Why? Are you having second thoughts?"

"Not a chance. I just like to know the deal." Luigi led the way inside their building. He trudged to the end of the hallway and stopped when he reached his apartment door. "Thanks for getting me a job, Mrs. G."

"You're welcome, Luigi. I think this is gonna be good for both you and Dernice. She needs help, and you landed a job that's right up your alley." Carlita wished him luck before returning home.

It was time to start tinkering with one of her Thanksgiving Day recipes. She slipped an apron on and then sorted through her recipe box until she found her mother-in-law's eggplant parmesan recipe. She wanted to give it a test run before serving it to her family and friends.

After preheating the oven, the first step was to peel and slice the eggplant. She dipped the slices in a bowl of beaten eggs followed by breadcrumbs. She finished dipping each of the slices and arranged them on a baking sheet before sliding them into the hot oven.

When the eggplant finished baking, she placed a single layer on the bottom of a baking dish. She topped the eggplant with spaghetti sauce, followed by a layer of mozzarella and parmesan cheese. She repeated the layering until she ran out of eggplant and sauce and finished with a heavy-handed dose of both kinds of cheese so that it coated the top.

The last step was to sprinkle fresh basil on top before popping it into the oven.

"Something smells good," Mercedes said as she wandered into the kitchen. "Whatcha making?"

"Nonna Maria's eggplant parmesan."

"You haven't made that in years. I'll be your official taste tester." Mercedes leaned her hip on the counter. "So, what's the scoop on the explosion next door?"

"It was an accident." Carlita told her daughter about the rusted propane tank. "The cops and firefighters checked the place out to make sure it was safe for Dernice to return inside. You'll never guess what they found."

"A booby trap?" Mercedes joked.

"You got the trap part right. They found a trapdoor hidden beneath an old cabinet."

"Leading to a basement?"

"I think so. Luigi and I helped her pull the cabinet out of the way but didn't have time to check it out. I'm sure Dernice will later. We also made a quick trip to Tybee Island." Carlita briefly told her daughter about the dilapidated property and the damaged door. "On the way back here, the car behind us bumped us. At first, we thought it was an accident until they did it again. They forced Dernice's van off the road and began waving a gun at us."

Mercedes' eyes grew wide. "Did they shoot at you?"

"Luigi never gave them a chance. He got off the first shots and managed to take out one of the car's mirrors."

Mercedes let out a low whistle. "Dernice better watch her back."

"She hired Luigi."

"Now that's a match made in heaven."

"I couldn't agree more." Carlita set the timer on the oven. "While this is baking, I'm gonna run down to the pawn shop for a minute."

"I'll keep an eye on it."

"Thanks." Carlita removed her apron before making her way to the bustling pawn shop. She sprang into action, ringing up several sales. Finally, the shop cleared, and she joined her son in the back.

"Thanks, Ma. One minute the store is empty. The next, it's full," Tony said. "You ever find out about the explosion next door?"

"It was a faulty old propane tank. The investigators aren't sure what ignited it. There's some damage to EC Security Service's front entrance door, but it's nothing that can't be repaired."

"Was anyone hurt?"

"Thankfully, no. Dernice had placed the tank by the door, planning to swap it out for a new one. She left right before it blew," Carlita said. "Dernice is having a rough day. Luigi and I rode along with her to Tybee to check out a property. On the way back, the car behind us forced her van off the road and the driver pulled a gun on us."

"Are you kiddin' me? That's nuts. Sounds like a case of road rage."

Carlita hadn't considered that. "I suppose that could have been the case. Before I forget, Dernice hired Luigi to keep an eye on the place. It's on a trial basis."

"Good for him."

The door chimed, and a customer stepped inside. "I'll let you get back to work." Carlita returned home and was greeted with the tantalizing aroma of herbs.

Mercedes was standing at the stove, staring at the bubbling dish. "I just took it out. It looks delish."

"I hope this tastes half as good as it smells." Carlita waited for it to cool slightly. She eased a generous spoonful of the layered eggplant into two small dishes and handed one to her daughter.

Mercedes studied the layers before sampling the dish. "You added your special Italian seasoning."

"Only a pinch."

"This is the best eggplant I've ever tasted." Mercedes polished hers off and filled her dish a second time. "I was thinkin' about what you said – how Dernice hired Luigi. Does she know about his background?"

"Yes, thanks to Elvira's snooping. Dernice confessed she already knew about his work history – or at least enough to make an informed decision, which I think is one of the reasons she decided to hire him."

"Luigi will be good at protecting the business."

"Without a doubt." Carlita slid the baking dish to the back of the stove. "We'll have to give this a chance to finish cooling before covering it."

Rambo, the family pooch, trotted to the kitchen and planted himself in the doorway.

"You wanna go for a walk?"

He extended his paws, stretching into a downward dog pose as he rubbed his face on the floor.

"I'll take that as a 'yes.'" Carlita stepped over him and headed for the door. "You wanna go with me and Rambo?"

"I'll pass. I was right in the middle of an action scene when the timer went off. Maybe next time." Mercedes returned to her room while Carlita followed the pup down the steps and into the alley.

"Hang on." Carlita clipped his leash to his collar. "Which way should we go?"

She was still contemplating their walk when a compact car zoomed around the corner and turned into the alley.

Carlita tightened her grip on the leash and watched as the purple-haired driver sped past. The car swerved into an empty parking spot right next to Elvira's car.

Chapter 6

"Looks like Dernice has company." Carlita and Rambo strode to the other end of the alley.

The driver cast Carlita a glance as she slung a backpack over her shoulder. "Hey." A thick layer of bracelets jangled as she reached inside the back seat.

"Hello." Carlita offered the woman a tentative smile.

"What?" The woman pulled out a gym bag and slammed the door shut.

"What?"

"Why are you staring at me? Am I parked in the wrong spot?"

"I...it depends. This is the parking area for EC Investigative Services and EC Security Services."

"Then, I'm in the right place." The woman slid her sunglasses on top of her head and studied the building. "It's a little smaller than Mom let on." She turned her attention to Carlita. "You live around here?"

"Mom..." Carlita lifted a brow as it dawned on her who the purple-haired, Volkswagen-driving woman was. "You're Zulilly."

"Zulilly Fontaine. You know my mom?"

"Elvira," Carlita said.

"Yeah. She's not here."

"No, she's not."

"Which is why I'm here. I'm here to help Aunt Dernice until Mom gets back. She's worried about her." Zulilly began walking.

Carlita and Rambo trailed after her. "You plan to stay here?"

Zulilly abruptly stopped. "You're asking a lot of questions. Who are you?" she asked rudely.

"Carlita Garlucci. I'm your mother's former landlord, not to mention her alley neighbor."

"Ah. I get it." Zulilly chomped loudly on her gum, her jaws working furiously. "You're the annoying mafia lady Mom is always talking about."

"Annoying mafia lady?"

"I wouldn't take it personally. Mom doesn't have many nice things to say about anybody."

"Your mother is a pain in the..." Carlita bit back the rest of what she wanted to say about her troublesome neighbor. It was neither here nor there and had nothing to do with Zulilly. "I thought you and your mother had a falling out."

"A falling out?" Zulilly adjusted her backpack. "Mom came to visit me in Hilton Head a couple of months ago. She was stressed out about a...personal matter."

"Wait a minute... Your mother visited you a couple of months ago and told you she was stressed out about something."

"Yep. Next thing I know, Auntie D is freaking out because my mom borrowed some cash from the business and left town."

They had reached Elvira's alley entrance. Zulilly turned her back to Carlita. She gave the door a sharp rap before glancing over her shoulder. "See you around."

"I'm sure you will." Carlita turned to go, but something told her to stay. She had a sneaking suspicion Dernice had no idea Zulilly was standing on her doorstep.

The door opened a crack and then opened wider. Dernice appeared. "Zu?"

The woman smacked her gum, a wide grin on her face. "Surprise."

"What are you doing here?" Dernice frowned.

"Ma said she was concerned about you. She says you're overwhelmed running the businesses. I offered to come down here to give you a hand until she comes back."

"Overwhelmed? Your mother cleaned out a bank account and left town. To top it all off, I found out she started a new business." Dernice pursed her lips. "I thought you and your mother had a falling out."

Zulilly jabbed her finger in Carlita's direction. "That's what she said. Last time I saw Mom, she said something about taking care of a personal matter."

"I thought she was depressed after seeing you."

"You thought wrong. In fact, we talked yesterday, which is why I'm here."

Dernice's voice grew hard. "You wasted your time driving down here. I've already hired someone to help me."

"I'm not leaving."

Dernice stepped out of the building and closed the door behind her. "You can head right on home. Call your mother – who, by the way, hasn't returned my last two phone calls and tell her I don't need help."

"No can do." Zulilly crossed her arms. "I promised I would stay here until she gets back."

There were a few tense moments as the women stared each other down. Zulilly reminded Carlita of her mother. She was a chip off the old block.

Finally, Dernice backed down. At least Carlita thought she was backing down. "I'll make you a deal. I'll let you in *IF* you get your mother on the phone."

For the first time since Carlita had met her, Zulilly's confident demeanor faded. "I'm calling Mom later."

"You're calling her now. I want to talk to her." Dernice adjusted her stance, blocking the doorway.

"She's not gonna like this."

"I don't care," Dernice sing-songed.

Zulilly reluctantly reached into her pocket and pulled out a cell phone as she shot Carlita a puzzled glance. "Why are you still here?"

"Because I can't wait to see what happens."

"Carlita stays. She's my witness," Dernice said.

The young woman tapped the screen and lifted the phone to her ear. "Hey, Mom. It's me...Zu. I'm here. Auntie D isn't letting me in the apartment until she talks to you." There was a moment of silence. "I'm not kidding. She's blocking the door. There's someone else here too. It's your neighbor." Zulilly rolled her eyes and handed the phone to Dernice, who promptly put the call on speaker.

"Why is Zulilly here, and what's this personal matter you're handling?"

"I can't discuss it right now." Elvira sounded distracted. "Zu was nice enough to offer to come down and help you. Don't give her a hard time."

Dernice cut her off. "I don't need her help. I hired someone to help me."

"Who?" Elvira demanded.

"Why should you care?"

"Because it's my business."

Dernice unloaded on her sister, ranting about her leaving town, how she was worried about her safety, how she left them in a bind after cleaning out a bank account. "And now someone is targeting the businesses."

"What do you mean, targeting the businesses?"

"If you had answered my calls, you would already know. I think someone has been messing around. I'm almost certain of it, although they haven't taken anything. And what's this about you buying a property in Tybee?"

There was a long moment of silence on the other end of the line. "How do you know about the property?"

"Because the deed came in the mail, and I opened it."

"Certified mail?" Elvira asked. "I told you not to sign for anything certified."

"It wasn't certified."

It was quiet again on the other end, and Carlita thought Elvira had hung up. "You said someone's been messing around. Is it possible it has something to do with the Garlucci family connections?"

Carlita's blood pressure shot up. "This has nothing to do with me," she snapped.

"Maybe they were trying to rob the pawn shop and picked the wrong business," Elvira said.

"I don't think so." Carlita resisted the urge to yank the phone from Dernice's hand. Instead, she forced her voice to remain even. "You've left your sister hanging while you gallivant around the countryside doing who knows what."

"This doesn't involve you," Elvira said coolly.

"It does involve me when someone is breaking into businesses in my backyard."

69

"Take me off the speaker. I want to talk to Dernice privately."

Dernice tapped the screen and turned so that her back was to Zulilly and Carlita. "I already told you. Someone broke in. They didn't steal anything. There was also a minor propane tank explosion, but I'm fixing the damages."

There was a pause.

"I'm taking care of it," Dernice said. "What's up with starting a new business and not even mentioning it to me?"

"Why? Fine. She can stay, but if she starts causing trouble, she's out of here. Good-bye." Dernice handed the phone back to Zulilly as she stepped aside. "You can come in now."

Zulilly smiled smugly as she squeezed past her aunt.

Dernice started to follow, and Carlita stopped her. "Wait. What did Elvira say?"

"She...uh. She said she'll be coming home in a few days. She said the Tybee property was an impulse purchase, and she's going to be selling it soon."

"You didn't mention the car that forced us off the road."

"No. I was so mad, I forgot." Dernice wagged her finger. "Elvira is hiding something. There's a reason Zulilly is here, and it has nothing to do with helping me."

"Now that Elvira's daughter is here to help, do you still want to hire Luigi?"

"I do." Dernice nodded. "I think I'm going to need him now more than ever."

Chapter 7

Carlita and Rambo circled several blocks before making their way back to the apartment. All the while, she mulled over Zulilly's unannounced arrival and the news that Elvira's abrupt departure was because of a "personal matter."

She found Mercedes sitting at her desk, staring at the computer. "Hey, Mercedes. What are you doing?"

"My computer is running an update, so I decided to borrow yours." Mercedes tapped the screen. "Did you see this?"

"See what?"

"I was doing some research for my new book. You'll never guess what I found." Mercedes didn't wait for her mother to reply. "I found a story about the investment company that's snatching up the Tybee Island properties."

Carlita slipped her reading glasses on and read the headline aloud, "Atlantic Deep Corporation is slowly buying up Tybee Island for their new project, Coastal Adventures."

Mercedes waited for her mother to finish reading. "One of the local businesses, a restaurant, caught fire after hours. It happened right before the owner sold to Atlantic Deep. I'm thinking about running over to Tybee to check it out. There might be a story angle I can work with."

Carlita remembered the car that forced Dernice's van off the road. "I would rather you not go alone. I'll ride over there with you." She changed the subject. "I just met Zulilly, Elvira's daughter."

"Elvira disappears, and her daughter shows up?" Mercedes slid out of the chair.

"You shoulda seen the look on Dernice's face when she opened the door and found Zulilly standing on her stoop. She wouldn't let her in the building until she got Elvira on the phone."

"Smart move, Dernice," Mercedes chuckled.

"There's more to Elvira's disappearance than depression. She claims she's handling a personal matter." A feeling of dread washed over Carlita as she thought about Dernice's brief and private conversation with her sister.

What if Elvira was up to no good, and Luigi was unwittingly placing himself in a bad situation? The last thing he needed was to start off on the wrong foot in Savannah and end up on the wrong side of the law.

They reached the lower level hall, and Carlita cast an anxious glance at Luigi's apartment. "I wanna chat with Luigi for a sec. I'll meet you by the car."

"Sure."

Carlita rapped on Luigi's apartment door, but no one answered. She made a beeline for the alley, passing by his car, which was parked in the lot. She rounded the corner and found Dernice and Luigi inspecting what was left of the business' front door.

"Hey, Carlita." Luigi took a step back. "Dernice and I were checking out the damage. I think a coupla sheets of plywood will secure the place."

"I've been thinking about Zulilly's sudden arrival and your sister's disappearance." Carlita crossed her arms, pinning Dernice with a stare. "Who does she think is messing around here?"

"She...uh...we aren't sure. I'm gonna go pick up some sheets of plywood so we can get the door fixed. There's a hardware store a few blocks away. I'll be right back." She hurried around the corner and out of sight.

Carlita waited until she was gone. "I don't trust Dernice, or her sister, for that matter. I thought working for their security company would be a perfect fit for you, but now I'm not so sure."

"You don't think I should work with them?" Luigi asked.

"It's just…" Carlita pressed a hand to her forehead. "I feel it's my responsibility to warn you that there may be more going on around here than meets the eye."

"Without a doubt. Someone's messing around the building and forcing vehicles off the road. This place is starting to liven up." Luigi patted his front pocket. "Me and my piece can take care of any trouble that comes our way."

Despite Carlita's misgivings about the matter, Luigi was an adult. She couldn't necessarily tell him what to do – not that she even wanted to. In fact, she suspected he'd handled a lot more dangerous situations than having the vehicle he was riding in forced off the road.

Zulilly sauntered out of the building. "Where's Aunt D?"

"She ran to the store to pick up some stuff to fix the door," Carlita said.

"I need to head out," Zulilly consulted her watch. "Can you tell her I had some errands to run, and I'll be back later?"

"Sure." Luigi gave her a curt nod as the woman slipped back inside the building. "Now her – I don't trust."

"I don't either." Carlita patted Luigi's arm. "All I'm saying is watch your back."

Zulilly and her car were gone by the time Carlita reached the alley. Her daughter was perched on their rear bumper. "I saw a chick with purple hair drive off."

"That's Zulilly." Carlita climbed into the driver's seat and waited for her daughter to join her. "My gut tells me there's something fishy goin' on around here."

During the drive to Tybee, Carlita shared her concerns. "Originally, Dernice thought the reason Elvira left town was because she had a falling out with her daughter, and she fell into a deep depression."

"Cleaning out one of the business accounts on her way out," Mercedes reminded her mother.

"Correct. My guess is she used the money to start a new company and purchase property on Tybee Island. Zulilly shows up on their doorstep, claiming she's there to help her aunt. Dernice is not happy about it and forces Zulilly to call her mother. From what I could tell, it wasn't a pleasant conversation." Carlita tightened her grip on the steering wheel. "I hope Dernice and Elvira aren't setting Luigi up to become involved in something unethical or illegal."

"We're talking about Elvira, here," Mercedes joked.

"Yeah, and that's my concern."

The Savannah River sparkled in the bright sunlight. Carlita rolled the window down, letting the fresh ocean breeze in. She breathed deeply as they drove onto the island. The hustle and bustle of

Savannah was temporarily forgotten as they entered "island time."

She slowed when they reached the main drag, passing by small shops and restaurants before reaching several boutique hotels, a sprawling shopping plaza and finally, the ocean.

"Check it out." Mercedes pointed to a bright new sign. "Coastal Adventures. Opening Spring 2021."

Carlita eased the car into an empty spot and joined her daughter on the sidewalk. "What's the plan?"

"I'm working on some general research. The new project might make a good storyline. A story along the lines of big business drives out small property owners."

The women began walking along a chain link fence. A layer of dark green mesh covered it.

Carlita stopped when they reached a section where the mesh was missing. A row of bulldozers, surrounded by piles of fresh dirt, was neatly lined up on the other side of the fence. "They're workin' on something back there."

They reached the end of the sidewalk and turned onto a small side street sporting an ice cream shop, a tattoo parlor, a gift shop and a bakery. A ramshackle two-story building was across the street from the bakery.

"Let's check it out." Mercedes crossed the street. She pressed her forehead against the window and peered inside. "This one is toast. It looks like a teardown."

Carlita surveyed the building next to it. There was a sign in the window. "Protected by EC Security Services. This is Elvira's sign."

"Her security company doesn't seem to be doing a very good job of protecting these businesses."

"Or are they?" Carlita pointed to the gift shop next door. "They're still in business. Might as well have a look around."

The interior of the shop reminded Carlita of the mom 'n pop shops in their old Queens neighborhood. It was eerily quiet, and the only sound was the whirring of the overhead ceiling fans.

"No one is here," Mercedes whispered under her breath.

"There has to be." Carlita paused to inspect a woman's visor. *Tybee Island* was sprawled across the front in pink letters.

A curtain in the corner rustled, and a woman emerged. "Hello."

Carlita set the visor back on the shelf. "Hello."

"Can I help you find something?"

"We're just looking around," Carlita said. "My daughter and I live in Savannah. We recently found out that a big corporation is buying up the local Tybee businesses to build some sort of tourist attraction and thought we would check it out."

The woman's expression grew grim. "We aren't selling."

Carlita shifted her purse to her other arm. "We're not interested in buying. We were curious to find out what's going on."

"All you have to do is look around to see what's going on."

"True." Carlita could feel the woman's eyes on her as she wandered up and down the aisles. Every time she looked in that direction, the woman was glaring at her.

She joined Mercedes, who was perusing a rack of keychains. "I think it's time to go."

Mercedes stepped onto the sidewalk and held the door for her mother. "Talk about cranky. She was giving us the old evil eye."

"You noticed too? I can't imagine glaring at potential customers is good for business."

They finished making their way to the corner and circled the block. Up ahead was another Coastal Adventures' sign, similar to the first one except smaller.

Mercedes stepped closer, studying the detailed layout of the proposed development.

Front and center was a boardwalk. To the left were depictions of carnival rides, shops and a resort-like complex stretching along a strip of sandy white beach.

Mercedes let out a low whistle. "This place is gonna be huge." She shifted to the side to read the description.

Carlita joined her, peering over her shoulder as she read about the Coastal Adventures' projects. "They're building more than one adventure park. There are plans for one on St. Simons Island." Her breath caught in her throat when she read the location of the third.

Chapter 8

"St. Augustine, Florida," Carlita said. "Dernice mentioned Elvira is in St. Augustine." The clues were beginning to add up. Elvira's disappearance. Zulilly's sudden arrival. Atlantic Deep Corporation buying up area properties. "I smell a rat."

"Something tells me Elvira is somehow involved in this." Carlita remembered the EC Security Services' sign in the window. "I want to ask the woman about EC Security Services to find out if she knows Elvira."

Determined to get to the bottom of Elvira's involvement, Carlita strode back to the gift shop. The lights were off, and the door was locked.

Mercedes caught up with her. "She closed right after we left."

"She sure did." Defeated and out of ideas for figuring out what was happening, Mother and Daughter reluctantly returned to the car.

During the drive home, Mercedes shared her ideas for her new miniseries. "I think I'm gonna call the first book *Shakedown in Savannah. Takedown in Savannah* will be next and the third will be..."

"*Breakdown in Savannah*," Carlita joked.

"How did you know?"

"It was the theme song for an eighties movie. Shakedown...takedown." She began to hum under her breath.

"And I thought I was being original."

The light turned green, and Carlita looked both ways before driving through the intersection. "Why don't you write a romance about a young woman from New York who falls for a former cop from Savannah?"

"Because it sounds boring. And you can stop hinting. Sam and I are getting along fine. He's happy. I'm happy. Our relationship is perfect." Mercedes' expression grew mischievous. "Why don't I write about a widowed mobster's wife and a pirate who fall in love?"

Carlita frowned. "Very funny. We're home. I'm gonna check on Tony to see if he needs any help."

"I'll go with you."

There were several customers inside the pawn shop. It took a minute for Carlita to find her son, who was near the front of the store, talking to a man.

"There he is." Carlita noted the look of aggravation on her son's face. "He doesn't look happy."

"Nope." Mercedes pointed to the open trapdoor, leading to the basement. "Tony was in the basement."

"Hmm. I wonder what's up with that."

Finally, Tony caught his mother's eye and made his way over.

"What's going on?"

"That was the City of Savannah public works manager. He said someone has been messing around inside the tunnels and wanted to check our basement."

Carlita heaved a heavy sigh. "I knew it was a bad idea to open the passage back up."

"Hang on." Tony approached the checkout counter and waited until their part-time employee finished helping a customer. "I'm runnin' down to the basement for a few. Can you cover?"

"Yeah. No problem."

"I'll stay behind." Mercedes watched as two more customers entered the pawn shop. "You go on ahead."

"Thanks." Tony grabbed a flashlight before making his way down the ladder and into the basement.

Carlita joined him. She perched on the bottom rung while Tony trained the flashlight on the brick wall. "You ever notice this before?"

"Notice what?"

"This." Tony pointed to a crack in the wall.

"It's a crack in the wall. I'm sure there are tons of cracks. It's probably a small settling issue."

"You're missing it, Ma." Tony shifted to the side and ran his finger along the wall all the way to the bottom. "It makes an almost perfect vertical line. Settlement cracks don't make perfect lines."

She stepped off the bottom rung. "You think there's another passageway down here?"

"I don't think so. I know so. The public works guy told me there's another passage on the other side, and you're never gonna guess where it leads."

"To Elvira's building," Carlita and her son said in unison. "Dernice showed Luigi and me the door. We didn't have time to check it out, but I figured there was a good chance she has a basement too."

Carlita turned her gaze from the crack to the padlocked metal door and tunnel. "There's no way I'm gonna bust a hole in the wall between Elvira's building and ours. Talk about opening a can of worms."

"As much as she likes digging around, I'm surprised she hasn't already found it," Tony said.

"Or maybe she has." Carlita told her son how Mercedes and she suspected there was a link between a new development on Tybee Island, Elvira's disappearance and her recent property purchase. "I also think there's a reason Dernice agreed to hire Luigi."

"You think they're going to somehow suck him into one of Elvira's messes?" Tony asked.

"It's possible. I warned Luigi to be careful."

"He can handle himself. Luigi's street savvy...even more street-savvy than Elvira." Tony helped his mother up the ladder. He closed the trapdoor and slid the bolt in place.

Mercedes wandered over. "What was downstairs?"

"Signs that there may have once been an access door from our basement to the one behind ours...Elvira's building."

"You gonna blow it out?" Mercedes asked.

"And give Elvira access to our basement? No way."

Back home, Mercedes made a beeline for her bedroom, anxious to jot down some notes for her new book, *Shakedown in Savannah*, before she forgot.

Meanwhile, Carlita sorted through her emails and began updating her renters' files. She finished her bookkeeping and changed into a work uniform to start her evening shift at the restaurant. The hours flew by, and there was little time to dwell on anything other than making sure the guests were happy and their stomachs full when they left.

Mercedes and Sam had stopped by to say they were going to the City Market to listen to Cool Bones and his jazz band.

Her daughter still wasn't home when she finished her shift, but Rambo was patiently waiting by the door. With a quick check for keys, she grabbed his leash and they made their way into the alley.

Mindful not to venture too far after dark, they circled the block, passing by Elvira's business entrance and the boarded-up front door.

She wondered what Elvira would think if she was there, and for the umpteenth time, wondered what "personal matter" caused her to leave home so abruptly. Was it somehow connected to her Tybee property purchase? It made sense since she'd cleaned out the bank account on her way out of town.

Was she hired to protect at least one of the Tybee Island businesses, but instead of protecting them, took a payout so the large corporation could target the owners, driving them out of business and then snatching the properties up for pennies on the dollar?

There was also the mention of the recent fire in one of the island's empty buildings. Surely, if the authorities had investigated, they would have questioned the other property owners, including Elvira.

There was a reason Zulilly was in town. Elvira had failed to mention to her sister that her daughter was coming to help. What if Elvira didn't trust Dernice? The woman was a convicted felon.

She hoped whatever was going on, Elvira and her sister would not drag Luigi into their shenanigans. The last thing he needed was to become involved in underhanded and potentially shady dealings.

"C'mon, Rambo. It's getting chilly." As soon as she unhooked his leash, he scrambled up the steps.

She caught up with him in the hallway and noticed Sam's apartment door was ajar. Carlita could hear the tinkle of her daughter's laughter. She gave the door a tentative knock. The laughter stopped, and the door opened. Sam and a flushed Mercedes appeared.

"Sorry to bother you. I wanted to let you know I took Rambo for a walk, and I'm heading in for the rest of the night."

"I'll be home in a few," Mercedes promised.

"Don't wait up for her," Sam teased.

"Sam." Mercedes whacked him in the arm.

"Ouch." He playfully pressed a light hand to his "injured" arm. "I'm just messing with your mom. She knows me better than that."

Carlita wagged her finger at him. "You know what I say. You better put a ring on her finger first."

"Stop." Mercedes made a chopping motion. "Knock it off. Both of you."

Carlita chuckled and winked at Sam. "You sure know how to get her going."

Mercedes was still ranting as he closed the door behind them.

Carlita shooed her pup inside and then wandered around aimlessly before deciding to get ready for bed. Mercedes still hadn't returned by the time she finished. Restless, she slipped her robe on and drifted to the balcony doors.

Her eyes were drawn to the building next door. There was a flicker of light in Elvira's kitchen window, and she caught a glimpse of a shadow darting back and forth.

Carlita studied the alley below. Luigi's vehicle was parked next to her car. She eased the door open and slipped onto the balcony. The faint smell of cigarette smoke wafted up. Although she couldn't see anyone, Carlita was certain Luigi was somewhere nearby.

"Hey, Ma." The balcony door swung open, and Mercedes joined her. "Whatcha' doin'?"

"Thinking about Elvira. Wondering if helping Luigi get a job working for Dernice was a mistake." The uneasiness she'd felt earlier returned.

"You worry too much."

"It's just…" Carlita tugged on a stray strand of hair. "Why didn't Elvira give Dernice a heads up that Zulilly was coming to Savannah?"

"Because she wanted it to be a surprise."

"Exactly. But why? Do you think it's because Elvira doesn't trust her sister? Dernice is a convicted felon."

"And Luigi hasn't been around the criminal element all of his adult life?" Mercedes slipped her arm into her mother's and led her back inside. "He'll be fine."

"I know…" Carlita's voice trailed off, unable to pinpoint exactly why she felt uneasy. "I'm headin' to bed."

"Tomorrow is another day."

"You're right." Carlita clapped her hands. "C'mon Rambo. It's time for bed. Where's Grayvie?" She checked the sofa to see if her cat was in his favorite spot on top.

"He's already on my bed." Mercedes pointed to the ball of fur curled up on her pillow. Hearing his name, he stretched and yawned before closing his eyes again. "Lazybones."

"Spoiled pets. Spoiled rotten." Carlita followed Rambo into the bedroom. He circled his new bed several times before finding a comfortable spot and plopping down.

Carlita waited for him to settle in before shutting the light off. She lay there wide-eyed and wide awake, still uneasy over Elvira's absence and the nagging feeling there was a reason for Zulilly's unannounced arrival.

She eventually drifted off, but it was a fitful sleep, her dreams filled with jumbled thoughts of Elvira.

She woke early the next morning, tossed and turned and then finally gave up on going back to sleep. Rambo met her at the bedroom door and let out a low whine.

"I know. It's time to get up."

They made a quick trip to Rambo's patch of grass and hurried back inside, anxious to escape the chilly morning air.

The pup abruptly stopped near the bottom of the steps and then let out a low warning growl. It was then that Carlita noticed Luigi's apartment door was open.

Rambo growled again, and Carlita tiptoed closer. "Luigi?" She stopped when she reached the open door, her breath catching in her throat.

Chapter 9

Luigi was seated at the kitchen counter, an angry slash across the side of his face and extending down his neck.

Carlita's hand flew to her mouth. "Oh, my gosh. What happened to your face?"

"Hey, Carlita. It looks worse than it is. I was bein' a numbskull. I thought I saw some lights flashing in my living room window, almost like someone was tryin' to see inside, so I went outside to check it out."

Luigi told her he caught a glimpse of a light across the street. "It was over in front of the real estate office."

"Just now?"

"About half an hour ago." Luigi winced as he gingerly touched his face. "I wasn't paying attention to where I was going and ran into a broken gutter."

"Broken gutter," Carlita echoed. "I know which one you're talking about." She inspected the angry scrape and dried blood. "You want me to go grab some bandages? I have some upstairs."

"Nah." Luigi waved dismissively. "I'm fine. It'll teach me to pay better attention to where I'm going."

"I was just out there with Rambo. We didn't see anything." Carlita talked with Luigi for several more moments until she was sure he was going to be okay.

As she headed home, another, even more disturbing, thought entered her mind. What if this incident and the other one involving the tailgating car had nothing to do with Elvira? What if someone from Luigi's past had tracked him down, and now that he was no longer under the protection of the "family," they were after him?

But how would they know where to find him — unless Ricco had tipped them off. Carlita immediately dismissed the idea. Luigi and his former partner, Ricco, were friends.

She couldn't rule out the Castellini family. Perhaps someone was settling an old score.

She kicked her shoes off and strode to the balcony doors. One of Elvira's motion sensor lights was on. Her neighbor's rear door opened and then quickly shut.

Carlita grabbed her cell phone off the counter and returned to the door, staring out as she dialed Dernice's cell phone.

"Hello?"

"Hey, Dernice. It's Carlita. You got a minute?"

"Yeah. Sure. I was gonna call you to let you know Luigi tangled with the broken gutter out back."

"I just stopped by his place. It's a nasty scrape. He said he thought he saw someone across the street."

"I heard. I checked the cameras but didn't see anything. I'm beginning to think all of our cameras are hunks of junk."

Carlita could hear papers rustling on the other end.

"I have something I want to show you. Do you have a minute?"

"Sure. I'll meet you in the alley."

Dernice was already waiting when Carlita got there. She let her in before taking a quick glance around and locking the door behind them.

"Where's your niece?"

"Asleep in the spare bedroom."

They zig-zagged from the kitchen and into the dining room, past Dernice's Harley motorcycle, which was parked next to the table before entering a narrow hall. There was a locked door at the end.

Dernice patted her pockets. "Shoot. I need the keys. I'll be right back." She darted down the hall and returned with a set of keys. She unlocked the door and flipped the light on.

An antique four-poster bed was in the bedroom, and the walls were covered with various pieces of art. There were landscapes with majestic mountains and blue skies. Others were abstracts...a half of a man's head, a trolley, the Savannah River.

A picture that looked vaguely familiar hung above the bed. "This is Elvira's bedroom."

"Yeah. You ever see her artwork before?"

"See it?" Carlita snorted. "She set my building on fire, working on some of her art."

"For real? Sounds like something she would do." Dernice crossed the room and opened the closet door. A black safe was anchored to the closet floor. She tapped the keypad on the front. The safe made a faint whirring sound, and then the door slowly swung open.

She pulled out a thick, manila envelope and handed it to Carlita. "Check it out."

"What is it?"

"Remember the mailman and the certified delivery he's been trying to make, the one Elvira kept telling me not to sign for?"

"Yes."

"After Zulilly surprised me, I figured whatever was coming in from the lawyer had something to do with Elvira's disappearance and her showing up. This explains a lot."

The envelope was addressed to Elvira Cobb. "Elvira isn't going to like us snooping in her personal business."

"Then, she should be here handling it instead of leaving it to me."

"True." Carlita reached inside the envelope and pulled out a thick set of papers. Her eyes grew wide as she scanned the top sheet. "What on earth?"

Chapter 10

"This is a divorce petition." Carlita studied the names on the paper. "Elvira Cobb and Greg Fontaine." She cast Dernice a puzzled look. "Greg Fontaine?"

"Also known as Gremlin. He's Elvira's ex, Zulilly's father and a weasel, although I guess that might not be the case...the ex part, I mean. He's still a weasel."

"He's petitioning for half of her assets."

"This explains a lot. No wonder my sister is freaking out. Somehow, the two never got divorced. Gremlin has decided to finally pull the trigger, and he wants half of what Elvira owns."

Carlita couldn't get past the thought Elvira had been...was married. "Elvira is married."

"Not by choice is my guess. There's more to Gremlin Fontaine than being Elvira's ex," Dernice said. "I started doing a little digging around. Follow me." She led Carlita out of the bedroom and into the office, motioning for her to have a seat in front of the laptop. "Check out his professional background."

Carlita squinted at the screen. "Managing partner at Atlantic Deep." It took a minute for the information to sink in. "Atlantic Deep."

"Which is also the company developing Coastal Adventures, the Tybee Island mega entertainment complex project."

Dernice continued. "Elvira is in St. Augustine."

"Right. You said you tracked her there."

"It's also where she and Gremlin were married. A coincidence? I think not. I think my sister thought she was divorced and found out otherwise."

"She heard about it from Gremlin or his attorneys."

"Or Zulilly." Dernice twined her middle and index finger together. "Gremlin and his daughter are tight."

"Maybe Elvira and Gremlin are working together." Carlita leaned back in the chair.

"No way. They detest each other."

"There's bad blood between them?"

"Bad blood is an understatement. Back in the day, Elvira was a lot more carefree. She and Gremlin were both big into the hippie scene. Course we all were back then...free love...peace. They married at the county courthouse in St. Augustine, which is where they lived at the time. Until Zulilly came along, life was good. Elvira's pregnancy changed everything. Gremlin wasn't up for fatherhood. He took off, backpacking across the country."

Dernice explained times were tough for the young mother and her daughter. "She filed for divorce, but Elvira had a hard time tracking

Gremlin down. She and Zulilly moved around a lot, going wherever Elvira could make a buck."

"Elvira cared for Zulilly."

"She loved her unconditionally. Zulilly made up for the bad stuff, the tough stuff, including us being abandoned by our parents when we were young. Then one day, Gremlin showed up out of the blue. Elvira and Zulilly were living in a compound somewhere in the mountains. He served her with papers, claiming he had legal custody of Zulilly. The jerk ripped that young girl right out of her mother's arms."

"How horrible," Carlita said.

"It broke Elvira's heart. She tried to get her back, but with no permanent address, no steady job, no support system, the courts sided with Gremlin, who had cleaned himself up, gotten a steady job and moved to Hilton Head. He refused to let Elvira see Zulilly, even with supervised visits."

"He sounds like a bad person."

"Gremlin turned Zulilly against her mother. It took years for Elvira to start rebuilding their relationship. Fast forward to now. Elvira, seeing a business opportunity, purchased a prime piece of real estate, not knowing her ex – whom she doesn't like – is part owner of the company looking to purchase it." Dernice placed the divorce papers inside the desk drawer. "I think Zulilly is here doing her father's dirty work."

"Why would Elvira allow Zulilly to come down here, with all of this going on?" Carlita asked.

"She can't tell Zu 'no.'"

"I'm still confused. If Elvira is in Florida, dealing with the divorce, how does someone messing around here, not to mention forcing our van off the road, fit into all of this?"

"I don't know. What I do know is that Elvira didn't want me to sign for those papers and now I'm regretting going against her wishes. Gremlin's attorneys can move forward, and she'll have to surrender the information regarding her businesses if the courts request it."

"What are you gonna do?" Carlita asked. "Are you going to tell your sister what you did and continue to let Zulilly hang around?"

"Elvira needs to come home. Zu needs to know we're onto her and that I know her father is behind all of this." Dernice placed her hands on her cheeks. "I hate to ask you since I know what my sister has put you through, but I'm at my wit's end. Will you help me come up with an idea for setting some sort of trap, a way to confirm my suspicions about what's going on?"

"I..." Carlita studied the woman's face. She had more than enough on her own plate – and her own share of worries. She didn't need any more. But the way Dernice looked at her, the look of pleading. The woman needed help, and Carlita was never good at turning people down.

She blew air through thinned lips. "Okay. I'm not sure how I can help, but I'll try."

"Tybee is the link. We need to go back there and take another look around." Dernice was booked with jobs for the rest of the day, so the women agreed to meet first thing the following morning.

*****

Carlita was up early. Since Mercedes was still asleep, she left a note before heading to the car, where she found Dernice already waiting.

"I'll drive." Carlita jangled her keys. During the drive, the women discussed Elvira's current location.

"I was up half the night thinking about the divorce papers," Dernice said. "I'm almost certain that's why Elvira was depressed and why she's in St. Augustine."

Carlita slowed as they passed by the gift shop Mercedes and she had previously visited. She circled the block and eased the car into an empty spot in front of a recently renovated building. A gold-lettered *Sales Office* sign filled the upper half of the building's large picture window.

"Looks like they just opened." Dernice reached for the door handle. "We should check it out."

Once they entered the building, they approached a small counter displaying several brochure stands. A dark-haired woman who had been sitting at a desk near the back wall smiled pleasantly as she crossed the room to greet them.

"Good morning." Carlita approached the counter. "We're curious about your sign out front."

"This is the sales office for Coastal Adventures. I'm Kim Turbell, one of Coastal's sales representatives." The woman removed a brochure from one of the nearby stands and handed it to Carlita. "We're in the early phases of creating one of the most exciting communities on the coast."

The brochure's cover sported an inviting picture of a sandy beach with shimmering water as the backdrop.

Carlita flipped the brochure open, revealing a map of the future development. "It looks like it's going to be a very nice resort."

"The entertainment complex will be a premier vacation destination. We have two more developments to the south. One is on St. Simons Island and the other in St. Augustine," the woman explained. "If you would like more information, you can jot your name on the signup sheet. You'll be notified of our progress and when properties become available for purchase."

"I guess it wouldn't hurt." Carlita scribbled her name and email address on the sheet. "I have a few investment properties of my own. It would be fun to own a vacation spot close to home. My granddaughter, Violet, would love it."

Dernice pursed her lips. "You people are going to ruin the tranquility and footprint of this beautiful island, causing congestion and increased prices, not to mention higher taxes. Elvira should know better than to contribute to the ruining of a beautiful island like Tybee by greedy developers."

"Elvira?" The woman's head snapped up.

"Elvira Cobb," Dernice said. "She's my sister. She owns a property Coastal is interested in purchasing."

Turbell's expression grew grim, giving Carlita the impression the woman either knew Elvira or had heard her name before. Or it could have been Dernice's reproach about ruining the island with big development. "I'm sorry you feel that way. Our company's belief is the complete opposite. We believe this will help enhance the community by bringing in money for more services as well as tax breaks for businesses and homeowners."

"And tons of cash in your pocket," Dernice muttered.

"Thank you for your time." Carlita grasped Dernice's arm, certain trouble was brewing on the horizon. She propelled her out of the building and onto the sidewalk. "I think she took your opinion personally."

"Did you see the look on her face when I mentioned Elvira's name?" Dernice glanced back inside the sales office. "They must have crossed paths."

"I wouldn't doubt it. Since we're already here, we might as well check on Elvira's place again. It's right around the corner."

"Hang on. I'll be right back."

Before Carlita could stop her, Dernice returned inside.

Carlita watched as she approached the counter. The woman frowned and waved her arms. There was a brief exchange, and then Dernice exited the building.

"What did you say?"

"I asked her if she knew Elvira, and she said 'no.' I think she's lying."

The women walked to the end of the block, where they found a row of abandoned buildings. A bulldozer sat poised to level the landscape.

"Let's go in the back this time." Dernice tromped between Elvira's building and the one next to it. The buildings were so close together, Carlita could touch both walls.

Clusters of weeds pushed up through the cracks in the crumbling concrete. There was a tall wall at the end of the narrow strip of land, separating the businesses from what appeared to be a residential neighborhood.

"I wonder what the neighbors think about Coastal Adventures," Carlita said.

"They probably hate it." Dernice slid a small window up. She snaked her hand inside and leaned forward. "I...almost have it." She let out a small gasp as the door popped open.

Carlita followed Dernice into the building. A small storage closet she hadn't noticed during their previous visit was to her right. She curled her lip and let out a gagging sound at the putrid smell of something decaying. "Gross."

"Something crawled in here and died." Dernice pulled her cell phone from her pocket and switched the light on. Pinching her nose with one hand and shining the light with the other, she stepped to the center of the cavernous space. "There's a peek a boo of the ocean I didn't notice before. This is primo real estate. Elvira could potentially be sitting on a gold mine."

They finished touring the interior of the building. Dernice checked to make sure the remaining windows were locked before they returned to the small rear courtyard. "I want to take a closer look at the cameras before we leave."

Carlita wrinkled her brow. "Can you operate cameras without electricity and wiring?"

"No. We have a couple of sets that look legit but are fakeroos. I spotted one the other day when we were here. They're almost as effective as the real deal." Dernice eased to the side, and something crunched under her feet. She dropped down for a closer inspection. "Uh-oh. Wait until Elvira finds out about this."

Chapter 11

"Someone busted the camera." Dernice lifted what was left of the camera's lens. The lens cover and a mounting bracket were scattered nearby. "Elvira's not gonna be happy about this."

"Should we report this to the authorities?" Carlita asked.

"To file a claim for damages?" Dernice tossed the broken piece into the nearby bushes. "There's nothing in here worth claiming. Besides, the camera is only worth about fifty bucks on a good day. Her deductible would be more than the cost of replacing it."

Carlita swept the pieces away from the door with the side of her shoe. "I don't see the point in damaging a camera."

"Unless whoever it was thought they might be recorded."

The women retraced their steps, making their way along the narrow walkway to their starting point. Dernice rounded the corner and nearly collided with the woman from the sales center. She took a quick step back and then did a double-take. "You again."

"We figured since we were here, we might as well have a look around," Carlita said. "We noticed some of these buildings are still for sale."

"Not for long. All of this." The woman made a sweeping motion. "Everything here is in the process of being purchased."

"Everything? What if one of the owners doesn't want to sell?" Dernice asked.

The woman smiled smugly. "They will. All of them will. It's only a matter of time." Her cell phone chimed, and she excused herself before strolling off.

Carlita watched her walk away. "She seems pretty confident the owners are all selling. Maybe she knows something we don't."

"I was thinking the same thing."

Thankfully, the trip home was uneventful, and there were no incidents of vehicles attempting to run them off the road.

"I think it's safe to assume the people who are still open for business are the holdouts and in no hurry to sell." Carlita slid out of the front seat and waited for Dernice to join her in the alley. "If Elvira's ex is as close to his daughter as you say, I'm sure he knows Elvira isn't around. Why bother having the attorneys send certified mail to her personal residence or business address if she isn't here?"

"Your guess is as good as mine. I can't worry about it any longer. I have businesses to run. I'm willing to help my sister, but I'm beginning to think she doesn't want my help. I'm sorry I wasted your time."

"I don't mind," Carlita said. "I know you're stressed out. Hopefully, Elvira will come back soon."

"And on that note, it's time for me to get back to work." Dernice climbed into one of the company vans, gave Carlita a quick wave and drove off.

Mercedes was already up when Carlita returned home. She was sprawled out on the sofa, the television remote in hand. "How was Tybee? Did you learn anything new?"

"Elvira is married. Her husband sent legal papers inquiring about her assets, and I signed up to get more information on the new Tybee Island project."

"Married?" Mercedes' mouth fell open. "Seriously?"

"Seriously. The attorneys sent a certified letter. I think Elvira is in St. Augustine, trying to deal with it. According to Dernice, she thought Elvira and her husband divorced years ago."

"Wow. I can't believe Elvira was ever married."

"Or that Elvira is a mother. Take your pick."

Mercedes hopped off the sofa. "So, what's this about signing up for information? Are you thinking about investing in a beachfront getaway? Because if you are, it sounds awesome. I would even volunteer to handle the management."

"The management company would be in charge of rentals, but I think the family would get good use out of a vacation destination." Carlita warmed to the idea. "It could be our mini-vacation spot, close to home. Speaking of home, I need to stock up on some groceries. I'm heading over to Colby's."

"Grab some of their pastrami." Mercedes patted her stomach. "I've been craving it."

Colby's Corner Store was a short trek from the apartment. Carlita stepped inside and gave a quick wave to Faith Colby, the daughter of the owner. She filled her basket, checking off the items on her list before heading to the checkout.

"Hello, Mrs. Garlucci. I haven't seen you around in a while."

"Ravello's is keeping me busy."

Faith smiled, the dimple in her chin deepening. "Dad and I ate there a couple of nights ago. We shared the family sampler platter. Everything was delicious and the portions were huge. We even came home with leftovers."

"The sampler platter is spaghetti and meatballs, chicken fettuccine and one more thing." Carlita tapped the side of her forehead.

"Shrimp in a garlic sauce over a bed of linguine." Faith smacked her lips. "It was delicious. Oh, and the bread was fresh from the oven. Dad and I polished off an entire loaf and brought another one home. Our server, Bella, even threw in some of your amazing butter sauce to go."

"I'm glad you enjoyed it. Speaking of the restaurant, I'm hosting a family and friends

Thanksgiving dinner there at six on Thanksgiving Day. You and your dad are invited."

"Thank you. I'll have to check with him. Last year we ate at a restaurant near the highway. It wasn't very good." Faith finished scanning Carlita's items and placed them in her reusable grocery bags. "When do we need to let you know?"

"Next week would be great." Carlita took the receipt and shoved it into her purse before reaching for the bags. "Tell your dad I said, 'hi,' and I hope you can make it."

During the walk home, Carlita mulled over Elvira's disappearance. Although the woman was working through a personal crisis, she couldn't envision her leaving Dernice with the burden of running the businesses for much longer.

Mercedes met her mother at the door and grabbed one of the bags. She followed Carlita into the kitchen. "You remembered the pastrami."

"How could I forget? It was the first item on my list." While Mercedes put the groceries away, Carlita whipped up a couple of pastrami on rye sandwiches.

Rambo waited until they settled in at the dining room table. Then, he parked himself in front of Carlita's chair and stared at her with hungry eyes. Grayvie, not to be left out when treats were involved, scooched in next to him.

"I have some for each of you." She tore off a piece of meat and fed it to her cat before giving Rambo a whole slice. "That's enough."

"You spoil them rotten." Mercedes took a big bite of her sandwich.

"So do you." After they finished their food, Mercedes offered to clean up while Carlita eased onto the sofa and kicked her shoes off. Planning to rest for only a couple of minutes, she leaned her head back and dozed off.

"The kitchen is clean. I'm heading to my room." Carlita jumped at the sound of Mercedes' voice. She covered a yawn. "Excuse me. I'm more tired than I thought. Thanks for cleaning up."

"You're welcome."

After she left, Carlita leaned her head back again and closed her eyes. "Maybe I'll take a quick catnap."

Grayvie leaped onto the back of the sofa and slunk along the top. He surveyed the situation before finding an open spot perfect for him and wiggled in next to her. Carlita patted his head, her eyes growing heavy as she dozed off again.

She wasn't sure how much time passed when she abruptly woke. She groggily gazed around the room. Something had jolted her. It wasn't Rambo. He was sprawled out on the floor next to her, sound asleep.

Carlita shifted her sleepy cat and did a mental shake to clear her head. She'd been napping for over an hour.

Ding. She was halfway to the bathroom when the doorbell rang. Retracing her steps, Carlita wandered over to the window to see who was standing on her back stoop. It was Dernice.

As if sensing Carlita watching her, Dernice looked up.

Carlita held up a finger and then made her way down the steps.

"Did you get my text?"

"No. I was taking a nap. I haven't checked my phone. What's up? Let me guess…Elvira decided to come home early."

"No. She's dead."

Carlita's jaw dropped. "Elvira is dead?"

"Not Elvira. The woman."

"What woman?"

"Kim Turbell, the woman from Coastal Adventures. It just came across the ham radio. Her body was found inside Elvira's building."

Chapter 12

Carlita blinked rapidly. "You're kidding."

"I haven't confirmed it yet, but that's the chatter on the radio. It's coming from reliable sources."

"This means…" Carlita grappled to understand the implications of the woman being dead – and the fact that she and Dernice were among the last to see her alive.

"I talked to Elvira a few minutes ago to let her know what happened since the cops will want to speak with her. And don't forget, you put your name on the information list, so the cops are gonna show up on your doorstep asking a bunch of questions."

A sick feeling settled in the pit of Carlita's stomach. Dernice was right. She had been one of the last people to see the woman alive, *and* her name was on Coastal Adventure's information signup sheet. Her name, her email address. "The police will quickly clear me. I just met the woman yesterday."

"But you do know my sister, who happens to own the property where the woman's body was found. That's not all."

"You mean there's more good news?" Carlita asked sarcastically.

Dernice gave her a dark look.

"I'm sorry, Dernice. My comment was uncalled for. What is it?"

"Remember when Turbell reacted oddly at the mention of Elvira's name? My hunch was right. They know each other. Turbell had been harping on Elvira, nagging her to sell. She called Elvira after we left yesterday."

"Maybe Kim Turbell talked to Elvira and stopped by there afterward to have a look around."

"Which is when we ran into her," Dernice said.

Carlita stepped off the stoop and began to pace. "It was a setup."

"In an empty building?"

"I don't know." Frustrated at Elvira's unwillingness to cooperate, anger suddenly welled up in Carlita. "Your sister is content to focus on taking care of her personal affairs while you're left behind to handle everything else, and now I'm involved."

"I'm sorry, Carlita. I thought I owed you a heads up." Dernice rubbed her hand across her brow. "I'm sorry for dragging you into this."

Carlita sighed heavily. "What about Zulilly? Interestingly, the incidents around here have escalated since she blew into town."

"She didn't kill the woman." A look of doubt crossed Dernice's face. "At least I don't think so."

"How well do you know your niece?"

"We're not close, as you can probably guess. I lived in California for years, and then there was that stint in prison, so we haven't kept in contact."

"Do you think Zulilly has an alibi?"

"Hard telling. She's been secretive about her movements. I'm not sure if she's working for her father or for her mother at this point." Dernice waved her phone in the air. "I have the address of the place where Elvira is staying. I'm almost positive she's renting a room in downtown St. Augustine."

"Send me the address." An idea started to form in Carlita's head. "I'm going down there to confront your sister before the police start pounding on my door."

"I wish I could go with you, but I can't leave the businesses unattended. I mentioned it to Zu about her going down to talk to her mother, but she didn't seem interested. I overheard a conversation last night she was having with her father. I'm beginning to think he may be behind some of this."

"The woman's death?"

"Maybe. Or whoever has been messing around our place."

"I'm sure I can persuade Mercedes to go with me." Carlita waited for Dernice to send the text with Elvira's address. After the text came through, she clicked on the link, and a map of St. Augustine popped up. "I have a favor to ask."

"What?"

"Don't tell Elvira I'm heading her way. I want it to be a surprise."

A slow grin spread across Dernice's face. "I like your way of thinking." She made a zipping motion across her lips. "My lips are sealed."

*****

Carlita promised to keep Dernice in the loop on her surprise visit before making a beeline for the pawn shop. After mapping out the location, she discovered it would take nearly three hours to drive to St. Augustine.

She would have to move fast. She needed to let Tony know she was leaving, throw some things into a suitcase, ask Autumn to keep an eye on the pets and last, but not least, convince Mercedes to go with her.

She was able to pull Tony aside long enough to explain she needed to have a face-to-face chat with Elvira.

"How long you gonna be gone?"

"My plan is to be back sometime tomorrow." She consulted her watch. "It's a three-hour drive from here. If I can convince Mercedes to go with me, we'll make it there by early evening. We'll get up tomorrow morning and track down Elvira."

"If she's still there," Tony pointed out.

"She is, at least, according to Dernice. I want to get out of town before the cops show up on my doorstep. If they come by here looking for me, tell them I'm on a business trip and should be back tomorrow."

"I hope this works out for you, Ma. You know how Elvira can be."

"Which is why my plan is to catch her off guard. Dernice promised not to say anything. In fact, she wanted to go with me, but someone has to stay here to run the businesses."

"Call if you need help." Tony wished his mother luck, and she headed upstairs. She found Mercedes working on her laptop in the apartment. She briefly told her daughter about the trip and asked if she would tag along.

Mercedes wrinkled her nose. "St. Augustine?"

"Yeah. I mapped it. It's only about three hours, straight down the highway with a turn toward the coast. We'll hit the road as soon as we pack some things. We can give Autumn a call on the way to ask her to keep an eye on the pets. If not, I'm sure Tony and Shelby will take care of them."

"Sure. I mean, there's no way you should go alone."

"Thanks, Mercedes." Carlita consulted her watch. The clock was ticking, and it was only a matter of time before the authorities tracked her down.

To her credit, Mercedes was ready before her mother and waiting by the door. Carlita wasn't far behind, after quickly cramming clothes into her overnight bag.

She plucked the keys off the hook and handed them to her daughter. "You're the more experienced driver."

"Not by much."

It was a short drive to the interstate. Mercedes picked up speed as they merged onto the busy highway.

Carlita cast an anxious glance at an eighteen-wheeler looming over them in the next lane. "What's up with all of the traffic?"

"Thanksgiving is next week. Everyone is heading to Florida for the holidays."

The women encountered even heavier traffic when they reached Jacksonville, creeping all the way through the city before making it to the south end of town. Thankfully, the St. Augustine exit was just south of the city.

"How much farther?" Mercedes slowed for the vehicle ahead of them. "We turned off the highway a long time ago."

Carlita studied her phone. "We're close. Our turn is up here."

"Do you have the address to where we'll be staying?" Mercedes asked as they turned onto the road leading to the historic city.

"Staying?" Carlita blinked rapidly. "Crud. I was so busy trying to get out of town, I forgot about finding a place to stay." She switched screens and began searching for area hotels. The ones near the highway were already booked.

She lucked out and found a vacancy at a bed and breakfast a couple blocks from the main drag. Carlita booked their room on her phone and slid it back into her purse. "Looks like we'll be staying in the historic district."

"It makes sense if that's where Elvira is."

St. Augustine's downtown area was packed with pedestrians and pedicabs. A trolley, similar to the ones in Savannah, passed them going in the opposite direction.

"This reminds me of home," Carlita joked.

"Me too. I would rather be walking." Mercedes slammed on the brakes as a couple darted onto the road and directly into their path. "People need to watch where they're going."

After making a wrong turn and circling the downtown area, they reached the inn Carlita had booked. Check-in was quick and easy. Their shared room was on the second floor. It sported a set of twin beds with an antique dresser separating them.

The adjoining bath was small but had everything they needed.

Carlita set her makeup bag on the narrow bathroom counter and limped into the bedroom area. "I need to stretch my legs, and I'm starving. Let's go explore and find somewhere to eat."

"I'm ready."

On their way out, they stopped by the small reception area to ask about restaurants within walking distance.

"Are you looking for something historic – perhaps maybe even haunted?"

"Yes." Mercedes clapped her hands. "The more haunted, the better."

"Then I recommend Scarlett O'Hara's. It's listed in the National Directory of Haunted Places and is rumored to be inhabited by the man who built the house in 1879. Make sure you visit the Ghost Bar upstairs."

"No." Carlita nudged her daughter. "Nothing haunted."

The woman chuckled as she handed them a map of downtown. "My second recommendation is Harry's Seafood Bar and Grille. The food is fantastic. It's two blocks up. You can't miss it. It's on the main strip."

Carlita thanked her for the suggestion and followed Mercedes onto the front porch. The Florida fall air was warmer than what they'd left behind in Savannah. "The weather is perfect. I don't even need a jacket."

Although the city reminded Carlita of Savannah, she thought Savannah's courtyards, the tree-lined streets and the canopy live oaks dripping with moss topped St. Augustine in the cozy charm department.

Mother and daughter found Harry's easily enough. It was busy for a Friday evening. They wandered past several tables to the check-in stand, admiring the lush landscape along the way.

Carlita added her name to the waitlist, and several minutes passed before they were led to a courtyard bistro table for two.

Mercedes perused the menu. "Everything looks delicious. A New Orleans' Style Restaurant." She read the menu's description. "We should try a local specialty."

While they waited for their food to arrive, the women enjoyed the balmy temperatures and acoustic guitar player. Their food arrived, and they sampled each other's dishes, both proclaiming theirs to be the best.

Carlita was hungrier than she realized and polished off her dinner in record time. After paying for the meal, the women wandered out onto the sidewalk.

"Check it out." Carlita pointed to the fort across the street.

"I read about it earlier. It's the Castillo de San Marcos." Mercedes studied the sign adjacent to the parking lot. "It's closed for the day."

"Crud. Now what?"

Not ready to return to their cramped room, they meandered through the historic district, stopping when they stumbled upon a walking tour in progress.

"...and if you're here late at night after everyone has gone home, listen closely. You might hear the bell ringing from the grave."

The tour guide, dressed in a long cape and top hat, motioned for his group to follow him.

"Let's see where they go," Mercedes whispered.

Carlita reluctantly followed her daughter as they trailed behind them. The tour group circled the cemetery before crossing to St. George Street.

The guide stopped every few feet to point out landmarks or give them a little history. Carlita found the most interesting stop was the one of the oldest wooden schoolhouse in the United States. It dated back to the seventeen hundreds.

"I feel like we should pay for the tour." Carlita pointed to a sticker one of the women was wearing. "These people all paid."

"We'll wait until the tour is over."

The group continued down St. George Street before crossing to the Castillo, the oldest masonry fort in the continental United States.

Spotlights illuminated the imposing walls. "The Castillo is one of only two fortifications in the world built out of a semi-rare form of limestone called coquina." He pointed to the spotlights. "As with many historic structures in St. Augustine, the Castillo is rumored to be haunted, in this case by an Indian war chief. If you tilt your head and squint your eyes, you may be able to see his profile on the fort wall."

Carlita nudged her daughter. "I don't see anything."

"Me, either."

The ghost tour ended on the sidewalk near the fort's entrance. Several people in the group thanked the guide, and a few even handed him a tip. Carlita and Mercedes hung back and waited for the crowd to fade away.

"We thoroughly enjoyed your tour," Carlita said.

"You were part of the group? I don't recall meeting you."

"We weren't." Mercedes shook her head. "We joined the group after you started. How much do we owe you?"

"I appreciate your honesty." The man removed his top hat. "The ticket booth is closed. I have no way to process your payment. We'll catch you next time."

"We would at least like to give you a tip." Carlita fumbled inside her purse, pulled out a ten-dollar bill and handed it to him.

"Thank you." He shoved the money into his jacket pocket. "Is this your first visit to the area?"

"It is," Carlita said. "We're here to track down a friend."

They made small talk before thanking the guide again and began walking in the direction of the inn. The women made several wrong turns. At one point, Carlita was certain they had made a complete circle. "We've been by here before."

"You're right. I think we need to go this way." Mercedes led her mother away from the touristy district.

They walked for a couple of blocks and then slowed. "I think we made another wrong turn."

"I don't recognize this street. Let's backtrack." Up ahead, Carlita caught a glimpse of the main road. "I recognize the street down there."

They were almost to the corner when a man stepped out of the shadows, blocking their path.

Chapter 13

"You got some spare change?"

Mercedes grabbed her mother's arm and sidestepped the man, attempting to pass.

He moved quickly, easily blocking their path, and a bolt of fear shot down Carlita's spine.

"I said...do you have some change you can spare?"

"No. We don't," Mercedes replied in a firm voice. "Step aside."

"I think you do." The man lunged forward.

Mercedes pivoted, jamming her elbow into the man's ribs.

"Oof," he grunted as he doubled over.

"Run!" Mercedes propelled her mother forward, neither of them slowing until they reached the main street.

Carlita leaned forward, gasping for air. "I never even saw him until it was too late."

"I think we were about to be robbed."

"He had no idea what he was up against. I'm proud of you, Mercedes. You kept your cool. Where's your gun when you need it?"

"Back home in my dresser drawer. We were in such a hurry, I forgot it."

Determined to avoid a repeat of the incident, the women stopped at the nearest open shop to ask for directions, only to discover they were heading the wrong way.

They were soon on the right path. Carlita and Mercedes didn't talk as they briskly walked back to the inn.

The employee they chatted with on the way out was still seated behind the desk. "How was dinner?"

"Delicious," Mercedes said. "We had a small incident on the way back. A man in an alley was panhandling and wouldn't take no for an answer."

"I'm sorry to hear that. It's wise to stay on the main streets after dark."

"We found that out the hard way." Carlita thanked the woman for the dinner suggestion.

Back inside their room, they turned the television on and flipped through the channels until they found one that featured the upcoming local events. "It's amazing how many similarities there are between St. Augustine and Savannah."

They watched the program until it ended and decided it was time to turn in. Carlita wanted to get up early to track Elvira down before heading home.

She waited for Mercedes to finish in the bathroom and then slipped inside to change into her pajamas and brush her teeth.

The lights were off with only the dim glow of the nightstand's alarm clock to guide her as she crept across the room to her bed. Carlita eased onto the edge.

Creak. The springs creaked loudly. She slowly lowered onto the side, causing the bed to creak again. "Sorry," she whispered.

"Mine is doing the same." Mercedes flopped over, and her bed creaked.

A small groan escaped Carlita's lips as she settled in. The left half of the mattress was lumpy, and it sagged in the center. She wiggled to the side to find a more comfortable position. It was a downhill slide, so she moved to the other side, all the while the bed creaked.

"You okay, Ma?" Mercedes asked after her umpteenth move.

"I can't get comfortable."

"You wanna switch beds?"

"Do you think it will help?"

Mercedes giggled. "No. My mattress feels like it's filled with bricks."

"Same here, except mine has needles sticking out of it."

"And my pillow is flatter than a pancake."

The women burst out laughing.

"This has been a day," Carlita sighed.

"It has, but at least we're together. We don't do enough mother-daughter stuff."

"You're right. We don't." Carlita slipped her hand under her head. "We're so busy at home with all of the businesses, your book writing, not to mention fitting Sam into your schedule."

"It is busy." Mercedes grew quiet. "Do you miss home?"

"We'll be back tomorrow, whether we find Elvira or not."

"No. I mean, New York."

"I…" Carlita's voice trailed off. Did she miss New York? She had lived there most of her adult life. They had only been in Savannah for a couple of years. Despite the short amount of time, Savannah felt like home, in some ways more than Queens ever had.

"I miss your father," Carlita replied softly, "but I don't miss Queens. I sometimes wonder what life would be like for us if your father was still alive."

"Pops would've married me off to one of his buddies' sons. I would have at least two children by now and be miserable," Mercedes joked.

"Would you…be miserable if you were married with children?"

"No. I mean, I want a family someday, but not right now. Pops never would've moved to Savannah."

"You're right. He was a New Yorker…an Italian New Yorker through and through." Carlita thought about her husband, his death and how much their lives had changed.

Looking back, she wondered how she managed to muster up the guts to sell the family home and start a life in a state she'd never even visited before his death. "Sometimes God has plans we can't even fathom."

"He turned bad into something good," Mercedes said.

"Yes, he did, which is why I find comfort in believing your father is smiling down on us. That he's proud of us."

"I think so too." Mercedes yawned loudly. "I'll see you in the morning."

"See you in the morning. I love you, Mercedes."

"I love you too, Ma."

*****

Despite the unfamiliar surroundings, the uncomfortable bed and Mercedes' soft snores,

Carlita managed to fall asleep and sleep through the night.

She was stiff when she crawled out of bed and tiptoed to the bathroom early the next morning. By the time she emerged, Mercedes was up. "You ready to get this day started?"

"I'm ready for breakfast first." Carlita remembered the woman at the desk telling them they served a full breakfast in the courtyard from seven until ten. It was seven-fifteen.

"I'm starving. Let me go get ready." Mercedes dashed into the bathroom, emerging in record time, dressed and ready to go.

The man working at the desk directed them to the formal living room, through the French doors and into the courtyard.

The courtyard reminded Carlita of hers, except this one sported tropical greenery, complete with royal palms, fan palms and a crepe myrtle.

Patio tables and chairs dotted the open area. A small sunroom was attached to the rear of the inn, and the breakfast area was inside the sunroom.

Carlita loaded her plate with a small sample of several dishes. On her way to an empty table, she filled her coffee cup and grabbed a wrapped set of silverware.

Mercedes wasn't far behind and set her plate of food on the table before pulling out a chair.

"What is that?" Carlita pointed to her daughter's plate.

"It's hot milk sponge cake with a side of Georgia peaches. Doesn't it look yummy?"

"It does. How did I miss it?"

"Try a bite." Mercedes cut off a small piece and handed it to her mother.

"This is delicious. It tastes as good as it looks."

Mercedes covered her slice with peach topping and took a bite. "Perfectly moist and perfectly tasty. You should try to make it, Ma."

"I need a more thorough tasting first." Carlita returned to the buffet and eased a slice of the cake onto her plate. She filled a small glass bowl with peach topping and returned to the table.

"It has a perfect consistency and the peach topping?" She rolled her eyes. "It's worth trying to replicate."

"It was my favorite dish," Mercedes said.

"Mine too." While Mercedes finished her breakfast, Carlita refilled her coffee cup and approached the woman who was replenishing the serving dishes. "I would love to get a copy of your sponge cake recipe."

"Hot Milk Sponge Cake. Of course." The woman reached into a small cabinet behind her and handed Carlita a sheet of paper. "The sponge cake is one of the most popular items on our menu. We get so many requests for the recipe we keep copies on hand."

"Thank you. I can't wait to make it." Carlita folded the sheet in half and joined Mercedes, who was waiting by the door.

Back in their room, Carlita realized she'd left her cell phone on the nightstand. She picked it up and glanced at the screen. "Someone called."

She didn't recognize the number, but whoever it was had left a message. Carlita entered her four-digit password and then held the phone to her ear.

"Hello, Mrs. Garlucci. This is Detective Skip Wilson with the Savannah Police Department. I'm investigating a suspicious death on Tybee Island. Your name has popped up as someone who may have information regarding the case." The detective rattled off his cell phone number and asked her to give him a call.

"Great," Carlita muttered. "Dernice was right. The cops want to question me about the woman who died on Tybee Island. I wish I'd never left my contact information. They're gonna start snooping around Elvira's business, find out we're neighbors and the heat will be on me."

"Again," Mercedes said.

"Again," Carlita repeated. "I don't know how Elvira manages to involve me in her problems, and she isn't even around."

"Speaking of Elvira, I think it's time for us to track her down. While you were getting ready, I downloaded a walking app, so we don't get lost again."

"That's a great idea." Carlita rattled off the address for Mercedes, who entered it into her phone.

On the way out, they dropped their room key off at the front desk and then stowed their bags in the trunk of the car.

Mercedes consulted her phone. "It's an easy walk. The GPS says we're only a couple blocks away."

"Elvira was within our sights even last night," Carlita joked.

"If she's there." Mercedes tapped the screen. "What is this place?"

"I don't know. Dernice said she thought it was a place that rented rooms. We could try looking it up before we head out."

"Nah." Mercedes waved dismissively. "We'll be there in less than ten minutes. Besides, I wouldn't mind burning a few calories after our delicious breakfast."

They made their way to the corner and turned left, walking until they reached the main road. They passed Harry's Seafood Restaurant where they'd dined the evening before.

Up next was the Castillo on the opposite side of the street and then the cemetery where they had joined the previous evening's city tour.

"Are we getting close?" Carlita asked.

Mercedes slowed. "We walked right past it."

They did a U-turn and headed back in the direction they'd just come from.

Mercedes kept one eye on the sidewalk, dodging pedestrians as she studied the phone. "It's the next building."

Carlita stopped in front of a brick wall, wrinkling her nose as she inspected the exterior of the two-story structure. A red covered porch faced the road and ran along the front of the building's second story. "Are you sure this is it?"

"Yes. This is the address Dernice gave you."

"This can't be right."

Chapter 14

Carlita shaded her eyes and read the sign above the double set of wooden doors. "St. Augustine Pirate and Treasure Museum." A skull and cross bones were next to the name.

"We might as well go in." Mercedes trekked across the courtyard and held the door for her mother. A gift shop, crammed full of pirate merchandise, was in the building. There were racks of plastic swords and buckets of gold doubloons. An entire corner was devoted to pirate hats and masks.

"Hello," the man behind the small counter greeted them.

Carlita echoed his greeting and said the first thing that popped into her head. "I've never been inside a pirate museum."

"Then you've come to the right place if you want to find out more about pirates. Would you like to take a tour?" The man didn't wait for an answer. "Our pirate museum is home to Thomas Tew's chest, the world's only surviving pirate treasure chest."

Mercedes' eyes lit. "A treasure chest?"

The man explained the four-hundred-year-old wrought iron chest was owned by Tew, one of the richest pirates in the Golden Age of Piracy. "Tew used the chest to transport his plunder from the Arabian Sea to Rhode Island in 1694."

"It sounds fascinating."

Carlita wondered if Pirate Pete had ever visited the museum. "We're here to track someone down. Her name is Elvira Cobb, and this is the address we have for her."

"I know Elvira. Is she a friend of yours?"

"I...sort of," Carlita stammered. "Do you know where we can find her?"

The man consulted the computer on top of the counter. "She's renting a room upstairs. I can't let you up there, but I can call her room to let her know she has visitors."

"Yes. Please."

The man reached for the desk phone. "Your name?"

Carlita said the first name that came to mind. "Zulilly."

"Zulilly," the man repeated as he held the phone to his ear. "No one is answering. She may have gone out."

Carlita's heart sank. "Figures."

"We can wait for her for a few minutes," Mercedes suggested. "Maybe she'll be back soon."

"We did drive all of this way."

"There's a side tenant entrance, but Elvira usually comes in and out through these doors," the man said.

"We're already here. We might as well tour the museum."

"Since you're friends of Elvira's, I can give you a twenty-five percent friends and family discount." He rang up the tours and waited for Carlita to swipe her credit card. "Would you be interested in searching the discovery drawers hidden throughout the museum?"

Mercedes leaned an elbow on the counter. "Discovery drawers?"

He handed her a pencil and a slip of paper. "There are secret drawers scattered throughout the museum. A skull and crossbones are inside each of the drawers. Find all of them, and when you finish your tour, stop back by here to collect your prize."

"I'll do it," Mercedes said.

The museum's entrance was on the other side of the counter. The dimly lit hallway was lined with glass display cases. Pirate's memorabilia filled the cases and spilled into the open room at the end of the hall. Long tables lined the center of the room.

Mercedes approached one of the tables and studied a book on top. "Book of Pirates." She plopped down and flipped the cover open. "Everything we ever wanted to know about pirates and more."

Carlita eased into the seat next to her. After perusing the books, they circled the room and then entered the main deck. A replica pirate ship, complete with a captain's wheel, filled the cavernous room.

"This reminds me of Pete's pirate ship," Mercedes said.

"I'm sure he's heard of this place. I'm going to take some pictures." Carlita pulled her cell phone from her pocket while Mercedes made her way to the captain's cabin.

They spent most of their time exploring "Shipwreck Island" and admiring Tew's treasure chest. The last stop was a small room sporting a collection of Hollywood pirate's memorabilia.

Mercedes, who had meticulously found the entire collection of drawers, returned to the counter to collect her prize, a replica of a gold doubloon. She slipped the prize into her pocket and turned to her mother. "Now what?"

"Elvira hasn't shown up yet," the man said.

The women stepped off to the side to discuss their next move. "We can wait a little longer. The only problem is, who knows how long she'll be." Carlita frowned.

"Maybe just a few more minutes," Mercedes said.

The entrance door chimed. Carlita gazed over her daughter's head and spotted a mop of familiar grey locks. "Guess who just showed up?"

Elvira locked eyes with Carlita. The look of surprise on her face was unmistakable. She stumbled backward, pulling the door closed behind her.

"Oh no, you don't!" Carlita ran to the door and jerked it open.

"What are you doing here?" Elvira tightened her grip on the knob, refusing to let go.

"We're here because you've managed to stir up a whole heap of trouble in Savannah. Someone forced your sister's work van off the road, tried to shoot at us and now a woman has been found dead inside your Tybee property."

"You're making a mountain out of a molehill."

"Dead people and a crazy person trying to shoot at me are making a mountain out of a molehill?" Carlita could feel her blood start to boil as she glared at the defiant woman in front of her.

"This doesn't concern you."

"A woman's body was found inside your Tybee property."

"Why are you here?" Mercedes asked.

"I...uh. I'm taking care of some personal business."

"Let's talk about your recent property purchase," Carlita said. "Atlantic Deep, the company that's developing the Coastal Adventures' projects, is partly owned by your ex...or should I say your husband?" She hadn't planned to let that little tidbit of information out and immediately regretted her slip.

Elvira's face turned bright red. "How do you know about that?"

"I can't divulge my sources."

"My sister," Elvira gritted out. "Now you're sticking your nose in someone else's business, even more than you normally do."

"Me?" Carlita gasped. "I'm a suspect in a dead woman's murder, thanks to you."

Elvira ignored the comment. "Who is Luigi? Dernice mentioned him when she called. Something about having him keep an eye on the place."

"He's an employee of yours."

"Dernice has to run all hires by me first. Wait a minute." Elvira's eyes narrowed. "He's one of your mafia men."

"He was a former employee of my son, Vinnie. Dernice hired him."

"She can't do that," Elvira blustered.

"She can and did. And now I'll repeat Mercedes' question – Why are you here?"

"I already told you."

"We're only getting half the story. This has something to do with Coastal Adventures and somewhere along the way, your husband, as well."

"Will you stop saying that," Elvira hissed. "I am not married."

"Others might say differently. Listen. I don't care if you're married or not. What I do care about is the police questioning me about Kim Turbell's death. I was one of the last people to see her alive."

"If you had been minding your own business, you would have nothing to worry about."

Carlita clenched her fists, resisting the urge to wrap her hands around the woman's neck. "You purchased a piece of property on Tybee Island, an investment, knowing a potentially large and lucrative development had started buying up the properties. Something happened. My guess is there are a few properties Coastal still needs to acquire in order to move forward with their project. You and the other sellers banded together, you came to some sort of agreement on a sale price and now you're holding out."

"Like I said, this doesn't involve you."

"Except for the fact, as I'll remind you once again, I met Turbell yesterday. Your sister and I stopped by Coastal Adventure's sales office, and I filled out a form. Dernice and I visited your property only hours before the woman died under suspicious circumstances, and now I'm a suspect."

"What were you doing inside my property?" Elvira asked.

"Dernice asked for my help since she can't get any from you."

The man behind the counter's eyes grew wide as he listened to their exchange.

Elvira glanced in his direction and then pushed Carlita out of the building. "This isn't the place to air our dirty laundry."

"Don't you mean *your* dirty laundry?"

Mercedes shot the man an apologetic look before joining her mother and Elvira.

"I need to get Zu out of there."

"I'm sure Dernice would appreciate that."

"Why?"

"Because she's a pain in the butt, just like her mother is." Carlita gave her a pointed stare. "She isn't helping anyone, including you."

"Gremlin." Elvira tightened her jaw. "The man is like a bad case of poison ivy. Once he latches on, you can't get rid of him."

"It sounds as if you two were perfect for each other," Carlita taunted. "Maybe you should stay hitched."

"As much as I'm enjoying my mother putting you in your place, we're here to get the names of the other owners whose property Coastal Adventures and Atlantic Deep is trying to purchase," Mercedes said.

"I can't help. I don't have the names. Besides, it doesn't matter. I'm not selling until I get my personal issue resolved."

Carlita sucked in a breath. Elvira was stubborn. She was also greedy. "How much is Coastal offering to pay you?"

"Two hundred and fifty."

"Thousand."

"Correct."

"That's a lot of money."

"It is, and I want to sell." Elvira tapped her foot on the ground, looking away and then looking back. "If I sell now, I have nothing to use as a bargaining chip with my ex. He'll have the property he needs, and he can still petition the courts for half of my businesses since we're still technically hitched. I have a lawyer working down here to get it sorted out."

"Why in St. Augustine?"

Elvira lowered her voice as a couple passed by on their way inside. "Gremlin and I divorced years ago. I tried to serve him with the papers, but he was MIA. After the required amount of time passed, the courts ruled in favor of the divorce. Unfortunately, my incompetent attorney failed to file the paperwork, leaving me still hitched to the jerk. I had no idea until recently. It's a technicality. As soon as we can get the proper paperwork pushed through, the divorce is done, Gremlin won't be able to touch my businesses and I'm free to sell the property."

"Except someone, maybe even Gremlin isn't willing to wait. Have you thought that maybe whoever is targeting you, the person who is messing around your businesses, killed the woman and possibly even planted her body inside your building to set you up?"

"I haven't had time to process the woman's death. What was her name?"

"Kim Turbell."

"Yeah. I know her. She's a nag, calling me almost every day about selling."

"The other sellers might be a non-issue," Carlita said. "They can just go ahead and sell."

"They can't. Coastal needs my property. If they can't get mine, there's no point in purchasing the others. They view it as a package deal."

"Which leads us back to the other property owners. I need names."

"Two of the properties were purchased in trusts. I only have the first names and emails since that's how we communicated. I was gonna do a little more digging around until I got caught up in this un-divorced fiasco."

"The authorities are going to want to talk to you not only about the woman's death but your Tybee property purchase, as well."

"Yeah. That might present a problem."

"Why?" Mercedes asked.

Elvira's eyes slid to the side.

"There's something other than the woman's death. You did something you don't think the authorities would approve of," Carlita guessed.

"Maybe," Elvira hedged.

"What did you do?"

"I was collecting a fee for helping one of the other sellers negotiate the property sale."

"You were acting as a real estate agent?" Carlita briefly closed her eyes and shook her head. "That's illegal."

"It's a gray area. I considered it more of a referral fee, but I'm not sure the authorities would view it the same way."

"For good reason. It's called practicing real estate without a license."

Elvira's shoulders slumped. "I wish I could dump that property. It's cursed."

"So dump it."

"Like I said, then I'll have zero leverage against Gremlin if the courts don't finalize our divorce. He gets what he wants when it's over."

"I think finalizing the divorce in exchange for the sale of the property he needs is a reasonable negotiation," Carlita said.

"Which should be the case *if* Gremlin was reasonable, but he's not. My guess is he's the one who's been snooping around. He wants part of my businesses, the property and to control my daughter."

"I thought she was at your place as a favor to you."

"And possibly to her father."

"This is an interesting turn of events." For a split second, Carlita felt sorry for Elvira, thinking she was divorced years ago only to find out she was still married.

"As far as the cops go, I have an alibi." Elvira waved her hand. "I can prove I was here in St. Augustine."

The door opened, and the museum employee emerged. "Is everything all right?"

"Yeah. We're fine." Elvira shooed him away. "You can leave now."

The man shot her a look of irritation and slammed the door shut.

"I want any information you have on the Tybee property owners," Carlita said.

"No."

"Yes." Carlita took a menacing step forward. "Because of you, I'm now a potential suspect. Kim Turbell died under suspicious circumstances. I'm not leaving until I get it."

Elvira mumbled under her breath as she fumbled with her cell phone. "I emailed it to you. Don't blame me if you find yourself dead. You can tell your mafia pal he's fired when you get home."

"You can't fire him."

"Yes, I can. It's my company, and I'll run it any way I see fit."

"Then stop hiding and come back to Savannah."

"I'm close to getting the divorce finalized once and for all. I need a little more time. I sent the information. Good luck with the cops." Elvira didn't wait for a reply and headed inside.

Mercedes let out a disgusted breath. "What a trip."

"Yes. She is," Carlita nodded. "Before we head home, I want to make one more stop."

"You want to check out Coastal Adventure's site here in St. Augustine."

"There's a connection between these properties and the incidents. Perhaps if we do a little poking around, we'll have a better idea about how Coastal Adventures operates."

"Do you think this is an inside job?" Mercedes followed her mother out of the courtyard. "That maybe someone who works at Coastal is responsible for the woman's death?"

"It's possible. I'm not ruling anyone out." Carlita's cell phone beeped. She glanced at the screen. The number looked vaguely familiar. "I'm pretty sure this is Detective Wilson. I'll let it go to voice mail."

Seconds later, the phone beeped again, notifying her of a message. She entered her four-digit password and put the call on speaker.

"Mrs. Garlucci. It's Detective Wilson from the Savannah Police Department. I would like to speak to you concerning the death of a woman on Tybee Island. I left a message for you last night and haven't heard back." He repeated his cell phone number twice before ending the call.

"I better call him back before he issues a warrant for my arrest." Carlita dialed the number. The detective picked up on the first ring.

"Mrs. Garlucci."

"Hello, Detective Wilson. I'm sorry I didn't return your call. My daughter and I are out-of-town. I left my phone in my room, and by the time we got back to our hotel, it was late."

"When are you returning?"

"This afternoon."

"I would like to stop by to discuss the death of a woman whose body was found in an empty building on Tybee Island. She's a real estate agent who was working with Coastal Adventures. The building is owned by your neighbor, Elvira Cobb."

Carlita wasn't sure how much she should admit to and decided being vague was best. "I'm sorry to hear that."

"Unfortunately, the circumstances surrounding her death are suspicious." The detective paused. "Do you mind telling me where you are right now?"

Carlita cast her daughter a quick glance, and Mercedes shook her head.

"I...what does that matter?"

"It doesn't, except for the fact that I'm attempting to locate your neighbor, Ms. Cobb, and believe she may be out of town as well. Have you had contact with Ms. Cobb?"

Carlita began tapping the top of her phone. "I'm sorry, Detective Wilson. We have a terrible connection. I didn't catch the last part. What did you say?" She jabbed the mute button and then disconnected the call. "I bought a little time with that stunt. It might look bad if Wilson finds out I met with Elvira."

"No kidding. I didn't even think about that."

The women returned to their car, and Carlita tossed the keys to her daughter. "The Coastal Adventures property is on A1A, across from Anastasia Park."

"Beachside," Mercedes said.

It was a quick trip across the Bridge of Lions. The road curved to the south, meandering past several businesses before ending at the park entrance. A large Coastal Adventures sign, similar to the one on Tybee Island, was beyond the park.

Mercedes slowed as Carlita peered beyond the sign. "Well, will you look at that?"

Chapter 15

"This place is opening next month." Mercedes parked in front of the Coastal Adventure's sign.

Beneath "Opening Soon," was December 2020.

"No wonder Atlantic/Coastal is itching to finish purchasing the Tybee Island properties," Carlita said. "They must have a small fortune tied up in this place."

A cluster of shops, each decorated in a beach theme, dotted the grounds. A Ferris wheel and the top of what appeared to be a roller coaster were off in the distance. "I wonder if there are townhomes and condos for sale here."

"The answer is a definite yes." Mercedes pointed at a cluster of pastel-colored townhomes. A "Selling Now" sign was front and center. A tall hedge of meticulously manicured shrubs edged the sides and back. "Let's have a look around."

They circled the hedge and stepped onto a section of sidewalk, which ran along the busy road.

A sprawling single-story building was beyond the townhomes, and a "Sales Center" sidewalk sign was near the front door.

"It looks like they're open." Carlita held the door and followed Mercedes into the building.

The man behind a desk met them at the counter. "Welcome to Coastal Adventures. Can I help you?"

"We noticed you have townhomes for sale and wondered if we could get some information," Carlita said.

"Of course. Please...have a seat."

"We're kind of in a hurry." Carlita tightened her grip on her purse. "I'll take whatever information you have with me."

The man reached behind the counter and handed Carlita a brochure, similar to the one Kim Turbell had given her. "Our prices start in the low two hundreds for a two bed, two bath townhome. The units increase in size and price, the closer you get to the water."

Carlita flipped the brochure open and scanned its contents. "We also noticed an entertainment complex down the street that's opening soon."

"Next month. Do you live around here?"

"No," Mercedes answered. "We live in Savannah and noticed your signs on Tybee Island, as well. Are townhomes available there too?"

"We." The sales representative cleared his throat. "Those probably won't start selling until sometime next year. This project is wrapping up first, followed by St. Simons Island, Georgia. Tybee Island will be last."

"Is there a contact person for that location?" Carlita thought about Turbell.

"There is. Let me find out who that would be." The man returned to his desk and leaned in to study his computer screen. "Kim Turbell runs the Tybee Island sales center. She'll be able to help you with more information."

It was apparent the man had no idea Turbell had died, which Carlita found interesting. "I'll be sure to check with her." She thanked him for the information and waited until Mercedes and she were out of the building before speaking. "He has no idea the woman is dead."

"Unless he just wasn't saying anything." Mercedes pursed her lips. "I'm not sure how helpful this trip to St. Augustine was. We couldn't convince Elvira to return home. We have no idea who owns the other properties on Tybee."

"It's not a complete loss. She did give us some limited contact information. I'm beginning to suspect one of the Tybee Island property owners may be responsible."

"I think her ex or soon-to-be-ex is behind the attacks," Mercedes said. "Look at this place. Atlantic Deep has a lot of money tied up in the Coastal Adventures' projects. I'm sure it's the same case on St. Simons Island. Elvira even told us they need the four properties to move forward on Tybee Island. Either one of the other owners is trying to pressure Elvira, maybe even going as far as trying to scare her into selling, or it's her ex."

"What if it is her ex? He would have motive and opportunity. If Elvira is out of the picture, there's a chance he could take control of her businesses *and* get his hands on the property. The only problem with this theory is the property could be tied up in court for who knows how long." Carlita tossed her purse on the floor. "It's time to head home and face Detective Wilson."

The return trip took longer than expected. They ran into traffic again when they reached the Jacksonville area. "Why would anyone want to live in this mess?" Carlita frowned as she stared through the windshield at the sea of taillights.

It was late afternoon when they finally pulled into their parking lot. Carlita, who had developed a headache, grabbed her bag from the trunk and rubbed her temple as she fell into step with Mercedes.

"You okay, Ma?"

"I have a headache."

A small noise caught their attention.

Dernice was standing in her doorway, watching them. "I've been waiting for you. How did it go?"

"We found Elvira. She's in St. Augustine, working with an attorney to finalize her divorce."

"She's living above a pirate museum. Which, by the way, is pretty cool," Mercedes said. "She wasn't keen on talking when we tracked her down, but she finally gave us some information. She seems to think Gremlin is behind at least some of what is going on."

"Because he wants her properties," Dernice said. "It makes sense. He forces her to sell to Coastal, divorces her and then takes half of her assets. But why kill the salesperson?"

"Money." Carlita shrugged. "Maybe money was the motive."

"Did she give you names or addresses?"

"I don't know. I haven't had a chance to check my email." Carlita and her daughter made their way inside with Dernice trailing close behind. "Why didn't she give me the information?"

"We're talking about Elvira here. Who knows? She also didn't strike me as feeling any pressure to hurry home. Back to the Tybee property, she was acting as a real estate agent, collecting a fee from one of the other property owners for helping negotiate the sale."

"Hold that thought. While I'm here, I need to chat with Luigi for a second." Dernice slipped past Carlita and strode to the end of the hall.

Mercedes headed upstairs, but Carlita hung back, curious to find out what Dernice was up to.

Luigi's door opened, and he joined them in the hall. "Hey, boss lady."

"How was the job today?"

"Boring."

"Good. Which means no bad news," Carlita quipped.

"The gig was smooth sailing. I'm ready for another assignment."

"That's the spirit." Dernice fist pumped the air. "I have another job lined up over at the civic center. It starts at eight Monday morning and runs all day. It's a cooking contest. Last year, they held it at the Savannah Convention Center across the river."

Carlita wrinkled her nose. "Who needs security at a cooking contest?"

"Last year, two of the women, the contest winner and runner-up, got into it. The runner-up claimed the winner should have been disqualified based on a technicality. The winner got a little hot under the collar and pushed her. She pushed back." Dernice smacked her hands together. "Next thing you know, it's an all-out brawl. Both women ended up having to go to the hospital, one to get stitches and the other with a concussion. There was a rumor about a lawsuit being filed so the civic center hired us to keep everyone safe."

"Sounds like something right up my alley," Luigi rubbed his hands together. "Can I bring my piece?"

"You mean a gun?"

"Yeah. I kinda forgot to clear it with you, but me and my gun are partners. We go everywhere together."

"Sure. I mean, they didn't tell me we couldn't bring weapons."

"Cool."

"Don't forget to bring the taser I gave you too."

"That thing couldn't zap a fly," Luigi scoffed.

Carlita laughed as she remembered the time she tazed Elvira, knocking her flat on her back. "Don't be so sure about that."

"Sure. I'll take it. You're the boss."

Dernice grinned as she patted Luigi on the back. "Have I mentioned lately I love your go-get-'em attitude?"

"Does that mean I'm in line for a raise already?" Luigi teased.

"Now I didn't say anything about forking out more cash. You're still on probation."

"I was joking."

Dernice thanked Luigi before following Carlita down the hall and up the stairs. "Do you think he would shoot someone? I'm not sure our liability insurance would cover an accidental shooting."

"He would shoot someone. In fact, I'm sure he has shot someone – perhaps multiple people," Carlita said. "What I do know is he's trying to...make a career change, so I don't think gunning someone down would be his first choice of action in any given situation." She thought about it for a moment. "Although I can't be certain."

"Personally, I'm attracted to a man who knows how to use force."

Carlita studied Dernice, and it dawned on her that she knew very little about the woman's private life, other than what she'd observed from a distance and what Elvira had told her. "You can tell me to buzz off if you want, but have you ever been married?"

"Nope." Dernice shook her head. "Too much baggage. I'm more of a free spirit. Besides, look at the mess Elvira is in with Gremlin and Zu. I'm not up for that kind of hassle."

"Some of Elvira's issues are self-inflicted. Let me revise that...*most* of Elvira's issues are self-inflicted."

"You got that right. I came close once...to getting married. His name was Kevin. I met him right after I got out of prison. He was a pharmacist on trial for illegal prescription sales." Dernice tapped the side of her forehead. "Kev was smarter than a whip but not smart enough to fool the feds. If convicted, he was gonna be in for a long time. I didn't want to put my life on hold for years, waiting for him to get out."

"That was probably a wise move." Inside the apartment, Carlita dragged a dining room chair away from the table and placed it next to her desk. "It'll only take a minute for me to check my email to see if Elvira's information came through. Can I get you something to drink?"

"I'll take tea or a Coke if you have it."

"Sweet tea, it is." Carlita filled two glasses and set them on the side of the desk before turning her attention to the computer. She waited for her emails to load before sifting through them.

Dernice draped her arm over the back of the chair. "You got a lot of emails. About as many as me, although most of mine are junk."

"Mine are too." Carlita slipped her reading glasses on and scrolled through the screen. She found Elvira's message and opened it.

There was a single sentence at the top. "Don't screw up my potential sale with your snooping."

"Sounds like something Elvira would say." Carlita clicked on the attachment.

Dernice leaned in. "What is this chicken scratch?"

"It is a little hard to read." Carlita slid the bar at the bottom of the screen to increase the font size.

TII – Remaining four Tybee Island Sellers:

210 Shore Street. Ken Gibbons.

212 Shore Street. Savannah's Beach?

216 Shore Street. EC Investment Group. Elvira Cobb.

219 Shore Street. Southern Holdings?

"I still can't believe my sister started an investment company. Like we don't have enough going on with the other two businesses." Dernice placed her elbows on her knees. "Nothing Elvira does surprises me anymore."

"Join the club," Carlita quipped. "Now, all we have to do is figure out who owns Savannah's Beach and Southern Holdings."

A legend, plus a diagram of the properties and their location were below the list of names.

"It's still hard to see," Dernice said.

Carlita zoomed in and studied the properties Elvira had marked. Her heart skipped a beat when something caught her eye.

Chapter 16

"Do you see what I see?"

"No." Dernice shook her head.

Carlita traced her finger along the screen. "Kim Turbell worked in this office, only steps away from not only Elvira's property but also the other properties for sale. An alley runs behind them, one where someone could easily transfer a body from Turbell's sales office and plant it in Elvira's building." She shifted in the chair. "Why was Turbell in Elvira's building?"

Dernice shrugged. "Elvira said she called her right after we left the office the other day. I don't know...to look at the property?"

"If we had the answer to why, we might have the who." Carlita drummed her fingers on the desk as she studied the diagram. "There's a link. Perhaps

Turbell was lured to Elvira's place, and the killer was there waiting for her."

"We still don't know how she died," Dernice said. "I asked Detective Wilson when he stopped by yesterday, but he wouldn't tell me."

"Speaking of Detective Wilson, he's called me twice. I need to call him back."

"The man is on a mission to get to the bottom of Turbell's death. Although he wouldn't tell me how she died, he called it a homicide, so there's a killer running loose." Dernice glanced at her watch. "I'm working on a small project I need to finish over at the house. Can you send me a copy of Elvira's email?"

"Sure." Carlita forwarded a copy and then walked Dernice out.

Next on Carlita's list was a call to Detective Wilson. She left a voice mail message and had disconnected the line when the outer bell rang. The detective was standing on her stoop.

She ran down the stairs. "I left you a message to let you know I was back in town."

"And I just got it while I was on my way over here. Do you have a few minutes to chat?"

"I do." Carlita joined him in the alley and closed the door behind her.

"Your name was on a signup sheet at Coastal Adventure's Tybee Island sales office. The sales representative, Kim Turbell, was found dead inside a property owned by your neighbor." Wilson tilted his head, eyeing her closely. "Speaking of your neighbor, she's in St. Augustine."

Carlita's scalp started to tingle. "She is."

"Do you mind if I ask where you were yesterday afternoon and this morning?"

"I was in St. Augustine, as well," Carlita admitted.

"Meeting with your neighbor?"

"Yes. It was a quick trip."

The detective reached into his pocket and pulled out a small notepad and pen. "What did you discuss?"

"This and that." Carlita nervously twined her fingers together. "Look, I filled out a form for information on a vacation property. I own income properties. There is nothing suspicious about filling out a form."

"Did you and Miss Cobb discuss the woman's death?" the detective probed.

"Of course, we did. Do you think I would be dumb enough to put my name on a sign-up sheet right before I killed the woman? If I were you, I would start investigating the property owners on Tybee Island, specifically the ones who are linked to Coastal Adventures."

"We are. Is there anything you would like to add?"

"Such as?"

The detective switched tactics. "How was Ms. Turbell's demeanor during your visit? Did she strike you as nervous, agitated, distracted?"

"None of the above. She was cordial, polite and professional. I left my information. When Dernice Cobb and I left the sales office, Ms. Turbell was very much alive."

"And where did you go after that?" the detective asked.

"After what?"

"After stopping by the sales office."

Carlita's mouth went dry. The interrogation...questioning...had taken a turn for the worse. "Dernice wanted to check on her sister's property."

The detective began scribbling furiously. "So, you left Coastal Adventure's sales office and went directly to 216 Shore Street, Elvira Cobb's property...the property where Ms. Turbell's body was found."

"We did," Carlita whispered, visions of being handcuffed and loaded into the back of Detective Wilson's car flashed through her mind. "We looked around and then left a short time later."

"Did you see Ms. Turbell again?"

Carlita could feel her knees start to buckle. Her hand shook as she reached out to steady herself.

"Are you all right?"

"I'm...I'm okay."

"I'll repeat my question. Did you see Ms. Turbell again?"

"We passed her on the street. She was heading in the direction of Elvira's property. She asked us what we were doing. We told her we were checking on the property. We talked briefly about the sale of the island's properties. She seemed certain the remaining owners would sell to Coastal," Carlita blurted out. She could almost feel the cold metal cuffs circling her wrists.

Detective Wilson's expression was solemn as he studied Carlita. She was certain he could smell her fear. "You've been helpful, Mrs. Garlucci. I'll be in touch." He left the last sentence hanging in the air before turning on his heel and returning to his vehicle.

Carlita's legs wobbled as she dragged herself back inside. She pressed her forehead against the door and closed her eyes. If the investigators fingerprinted the inside of Elvira's building, her prints would be there. Her prints. Dernice's prints.

Carlita took a deep breath. There was nothing she could do. She *had* visited the sales office. She *had* stopped by Elvira's place. They had run into the woman again.

She forced Detective Wilson's visit from her mind and finished going over her books from yesterday before heading to Ravello's.

Her next stop was the pawn shop, where she found her daughter-in-law, Shelby, working. She caught Carlita's eye and met her near the back. "Hello, Carlita. How was St. Augustine?"

"Eventful. We tracked Elvira down. She's working on finalizing her divorce."

"I had no idea she was married," Shelby chuckled.

"It's a long story," Carlita sighed.

The women made small talk until a customer arrived, and Shelby excused herself.

On her way out, Carlita noticed the basement trapdoor was unlocked. She returned to the store floor to ask Tony about it, but he was busy helping a customer.

Carlita made her way back to the trapdoor. She reached for the door to flip it shut when she changed her mind. Instead, she decided to have a look around, remembering Elvira's trapdoor and how Tony had mentioned the brick wall and an entrance to Elvira's building.

She grabbed a flashlight and cautiously made her way down the ladder. She paused when she reached the bottom step, checking for critters. Carlita finished her descent and approached the far wall.

Small piles of loose concrete lined the bottom. She pinched some between her fingers and watched it fall.

Carlita dusted her hands and wandered over to the gate to make sure the padlock was secure.

Tink.

She spun around, shining her light into the tunnel. The tunnel was empty.

"Hmm." Carlita shifted the flashlight to her other hand.

Tink.

"I know I'm not losing my mind."

Tink.

Carlita backtracked, returning to the wall. Small bits of concrete fell to the floor, adding to the small pile. *Tink.*

"Dernice Cobb." Carlita scrambled up the ladder. She slammed the trapdoor shut and marched out of the pawn shop, not stopping until she reached her neighbor's back door. She pounded loudly. No one answered, and she guessed it was because Dernice was in the basement and couldn't hear.

Carlita hustled around the block and into EC Security Services' office. A petite, brown-haired woman sat behind the desk. "Can I help you?"

"I need to talk to Dernice." Carlita strode through the office area and into the back. The trapdoor Luigi and she had helped uncover was wide open.

"Dernice?" Carlita hollered as she descended the ladder. She found her neighbor standing next to the wall, holding a sledgehammer.

Whack. Dernice lifted the sledgehammer and swung at the wall, causing chunks of brick to fall to the floor.

"Dernice."

"Huh?" Dernice removed her earplugs and stumbled back. "Carlita. What're you doing here?"

"Stopping you from knocking a hole in my basement wall."

"Your wall?" Dernice shoved her safety goggles to her forehead.

"You're busting your way into my basement. I can hear you on the other side."

"Your basement is on the other side of this wall?"

"It is, and I would appreciate it if you would leave the wall up."

"I..." Dernice blinked rapidly. "I figured this led to another tunnel."

"It does, in a roundabout way, via my basement."

"I'm sorry, Carlita."

"It's okay. I...just think it's best if we keep a wall between us." Carlita studied the basement. It was similar to hers in both size and layout. On the opposite wall was a narrow tunnel. "There's a tunnel over there. Have you checked it out yet?"

"I went a few feet in. I wasn't armed, so I didn't go far. I'm trying to figure out if I should board it up or leave it open. Either way, Elvira won't be happy if I do too much messing around down here."

"You're probably right."

"I was gonna go explore after I finished busting through." Dernice propped the sledgehammer against the ladder. "You want to check it out?"

"Sure." Carlita waited in the basement while Dernice ran back upstairs to grab a taser and another flashlight.

When she returned, she handed Carlita the extra flashlight. "I've been doing some research on the tunnels. If these walls could talk, they would have a lot to say. From what I learned, everything from bodies during the yellow fever epidemic to whiskey during prohibition was transported through here."

"Pete Taylor told me the pirates used them too. The Parrot House has been in Pete's family for hundreds of years. The bar's owner, Pete's great-great-great something, would offer free rounds of rum to the local men. After they got drunk and passed out, the ship's crew would carry them through the tunnels to the waiting pirate ships. By the time the men woke up, they were at sea and used as free labor until the return trip."

"It's called shanghaiing. I read about it," Dernice said. "I wonder if there's any buried treasure down here."

Carlita thought about the gems and Mrs. Alder's body she and her children found hidden in the tunnel wall just outside her basement. "Buried treasure? Maybe. Buried bodies? Definitely."

"Daylight is burning." Dernice checked her flashlight and then beamed it in the direction of the tunnel's entrance. "Time to check it out."

Chapter 17

The tunnel was narrower, and the ceiling lower than Carlita's. "This must be a secondary tunnel. The one connecting to mine is larger than this."

The tunnel narrowed even more, forcing the women to hunch over as they inched forward. It abruptly ended and "t'd" off in opposite directions.

Dernice shined her flashlight to the left and then the right. "Which way should we go?"

"I'm not sure. You can't go wrong with right."

"To the right, it is."

They continued creeping along, mindful of the uneven ground. Every few feet, Carlita batted at a cobweb. The musty smell she'd noticed near the entrance to the tunnel grew stronger with every step they took. The damp air hung heavy, and an occasional *tink* made her skin crawl.

Dernice must've thought the same. "That noise is freaking me out. I wonder if there are tunnel rats down here."

"I'm sure, but hopefully not the size of the rats in New York." While they crept along, Carlita thought about Savannah's history and tried to envision what it would have been like to live in the vibrant city in the eighteen hundreds.

She hadn't spent much time researching Savannah's history and, in fact, vowed to take one of Sam's Savannah tours one day.

The tunnel ended at another brick wall. The women retraced their steps, passing by the entrance leading to Elvira's basement. The left tunnel went even farther. There was a metal gate at the end.

"It's the end of the road." Dernice tapped the rusted padlock securing the entrance.

"Or at least the end of our tunnel exploring." Carlita had turned to go when she spied a brick jutting out of the wall. Her eyes traveled up the side. A foot above the first brick was another and then another. "Check it out."

Dernice shined her flashlight along the bricks. There was a trapdoor at the top. "It looks old."

"Like it's been here for a very long time," Carlita agreed.

Dernice stepped onto the bottom brick.

"What are you doing?"

"Finding out what's up there."

"Someone else's property. That's what's up there."

Dernice ignored the comment and handed Carlita her flashlight. "Hold this." She balanced on one foot and gripped an upper brick with both hands. It was a slow go as she inched up the side. She reached the top "rung," ducking her head to keep from hitting it on the door.

"This might not be a good idea," Carlita warned.

Dernice adjusted her grip. Balancing her left foot on the narrow brick, she cautiously raised her right hand over her head and began pushing on the door. It made a loud popping sound but refused to budge.

"It could be locked from the inside."

"Maybe." Dernice, determined to find out what was on the other side, pushed again, this time harder.

Carlita caught a glimpse of a beam of light. "You're making progress."

She pushed a third time, and the door popped up. "Here goes nothing." Dernice balanced on the tips of her toes. She crouched down and then sprang straight up. The upper half of her body disappeared, leaving both feet dangling in the air.

She paddled furiously until her shoe made contact with the side of the trapdoor. Using her foot as leverage, she dragged the rest of her body through the opening and rolled out of sight.

She reappeared moments later, sticking her head in the opening. "Are you coming up?"

"We're trespassing."

"I call it exploring." She snapped her fingers. "Throw me my flashlight."

Carlita tossed the flashlight in the air, and Dernice easily caught it. "Thanks. Call 911 if I don't come back in five minutes."

"There's no cell reception in an underground tunnel."

"Then, run for your life." Dernice moved away from the opening.

The floor creaked overhead and then it grew quiet.

Carlita stepped directly beneath the open door. She cupped her hands to her mouth. "Are you okay?"

"Ack."

"Dernice!"

There was no answer.

"Good grief." Carlita reluctantly climbed the makeshift ladder, slowing when she reached the top. "Dernice?"

"Yeah." Dernice spun around, shining the light in Carlita's eyes.

Carlita flung her arm across her face. "Hey."

"Sorry." The beam lowered. "You changed your mind?"

"No. I heard you scream. I wanted to make sure you were all right."

"I'm fine. Something scuttled across my shoe. It's gone now. The place is empty."

"Are you sure?"

"Yep." Dernice gave her a hand up.

There was a dull beam of light coming in through a small window. Cardboard boxes sat beneath the window. A copper sink and a cast-iron, woodburning stove was on the opposite side of the room.

"This place has been vacant for a while." Dernice blew on the top of a nearby box, sending a cloud of dust into the air.

"I wonder where we are." Carlita tiptoed to the grungy window and peered out. The only thing visible was a brick wall.

Dernice trudged across the room.

"We shouldn't be in here."

"I think this is an old store." Dernice stepped behind a counter to admire a bar mirror that ran the entire length. Wooden shelves were below the mirror, and a galley-style walkway separated the shelves from a long gray-green Formica counter. "Or maybe it was an ice cream shop."

A faint *click* echoed from somewhere behind the counter seconds before the wail of a security alarm filled the air.

"We tripped the alarm." Carlita dashed across the room. Dernice was right behind her. The women reached the trapdoor at the same time.

Dernice shoved Carlita out of the way and flew down the makeshift ladder.

She lost her footing halfway down and fell the rest of the way, landing flat on her back.

"Are you all right?"

"I'm fine." Dernice scrambled to her feet. "Hurry up!"

"I'm trying." Carlita inched her way to the bottom, determined to avoid the fall Dernice had taken. She stopped halfway and pulled the trapdoor shut before finishing her descent. "I can't believe I came after you to make sure you were all right and then you push me out of the way to save your own hide."

"Sorry. I had the fight or flight instinct."

Carlita rolled her eyes. "I've had enough fun for today."

The women were silent as they made a quick trek back to Elvira's basement. Carlita climbed the ladder and waited for Dernice to join her. "I would install some sort of barricade or a door if I were you."

"If not, we'll have people snooping around here like we just did."

"Exactly."

Dernice dropped the door in place and slid the bolt to secure it. "I got to thinking about Elvira's list. One of the names sounded familiar."

"Which one?" Carlita asked.

"Southern Holdings. I'm going to research my customer database to see if there's a match."

The women stopped by the kitchen to wash their hands in the sink before making their way to the office.

Zulilly was seated at one of the desks, her back to them.

Dernice tapped her on the shoulder and made a sweeping motion with her hands.

"What?" Zulilly frowned.

"Out. Get out of my chair."

"This isn't your chair. It's my mother's chair. The chair and everything else in here is hers."

"You're a royal pain. Why don't you go home? You're in the way."

"Because my mother wants me here. I'm not going anywhere."

"You're going...you're going to get out of my chair." Dernice whacked the back, jarring the chair's occupant. "Out."

Zulilly flipped her purple locks off her shoulder and made a hissing sound as she slid out of the chair. She flung herself into the chair across from Dernice and glared at her aunt.

"Glare at me all you want." Dernice turned her attention to the computer. "Stop playing solitaire on my computer."

Zulilly ignored the comment. She snatched an ink pen off the desk and began clicking the end.

Dernice clenched her jaw. "Do you have to do that?" she gritted out.

"Is it aggravating you?"

"What do you think?"

"I think that's why I'm doing it." Zulilly continued clicking the pen. Click. Click. Click. Click.

Dernice tapped the keyboard and ignored the clicks. "I think I figured it out," she finally said.

"You did?" Carlita hurried to her side.

"Figured what out?" Zulilly stopped clicking.

"None of your beeswax."

"You're a witch." Zulilly slid out of the chair and stomped out of the office. She slammed the front door on her way out.

Dernice paused long enough to watch Zulilly pass by the front window. "She's a chip off the old block."

"I'm afraid you're right," Carlita patted Dernice's arm. "I thought you were going to rip the pen out of her hand and stab her with it," she joked.

"Now that's an idea. I wish she would go home. I'm hardly able to say anything to her without her crying to her mother about how mean Auntie D is." Dernice sighed heavily. "I want to make it through the next few days, for Elvira to come home and life return to normal."

"Can you have a normal life living with Elvira?" Carlita couldn't help herself.

"True." Dernice tapped the computer screen. "I found Southern Holdings. Remember how I said I thought the name sounded familiar? We quoted a job for the owner a couple months ago."

Carlita squinted her eyes. "It's hard to read. I don't have my reading glasses."

"I'll print out the quote."

The printer behind Dernice hummed. A single sheet of paper appeared. She plucked it from the tray and handed it to Carlita.

Carlita's eyes scanned the sheet. At first, she didn't see it, until she got to the very bottom where it listed not only Southern Holdings, but also the name of the company's owner.

Chapter 18

"Victoria Montgomery," Carlita whispered. "There's no way Tori is involved in Kim Turbell's death."

"Victoria Montgomery." Dernice repeated the name. "She's the lady who caught Elvira sneaking onto her property. She called the cops and my sister ended up in jail."

"That's her. Tori owns a small gift shop on Tybee Island." Carlita began to pace. "Tori has lived on the island for years. She might know who owns the other company, Savannah's Beach." Carlita headed to the door.

"Are you going to her place?" Dernice jumped out of the chair and hurried after her. "Can I go with you?"

"Yes. Maybe. I'll have to call her first." Carlita promised to let her know what Tori said and then returned home. After checking on Mercedes, she took Rambo for a walk to clear her head.

True, Tori had a colorful history and background, but Carlita was certain she wasn't involved in strong-armed tactics designed to force Elvira or any of the other property owners to sell. Still, Tori's past was, in some ways, as checkered as Carlita's.

Over the years, the savvy businesswoman and her husband had not only amassed a small fortune, but they had also built Montgomery Hall, a massive estate encompassing a corner of the island. She also owned Summer Sparkle, a gift and jewelry shop on the island. Apparently, she owned other real estate, as well.

She mentally reviewed the list of possible suspects as they walked. Tori and Southern Holdings were off the list. Although Elvira was annoying, Carlita didn't think she was capable of murder, at least not intentionally. Besides, she had an airtight alibi. Unless...she had hired someone to kill the woman, but what would be her motive? Plus, Elvira wouldn't be dumb enough to leave the woman's body inside a property she owned.

Up next was Ken Gibbons, another property owner. Last, but not least, was whoever owned Savannah's Beach. Which is where a chat with Tori came in. If anyone knew who owned the company, it would be her.

They circled the block, passing by the Book Nook, the meeting spot for Mercedes' local author group. Cricket Tidwell, the owner, stood in the doorway chatting with a woman.

Carlita gave her a friendly wave. They passed by Colby's Corner Store just down the street before turning the corner.

Shades of Ink, Steve Winter's tattoo shop, was up next. Steve was inside, near the large front window, talking on his cell phone. He caught Carlita's eye and motioned for her to wait.

"Hold on, Rambo." Carlita gave Rambo's leash a gentle tug. "Steve wants to say hello."

He stepped onto the sidewalk. "Hey, Carlita."

"Hello, Steve. How's business these days?"

"Business is booming. It looks like the pawn shop is rocking too."

"It is, and so is Ravello's. Speaking of Ravello's, have you had a chance to ask Paisley about joining us for Thanksgiving dinner?"

"Yeah. That's why I stopped you. We'll be there."

"Autumn, is coming, too."

"Yep." Steve shifted his feet as he nodded toward her buildings. "What happened the other day?"

"Which time?"

"The firefighters. Kaboom." Steve's hands flew in the air. "The explosion at Elvira's place."

"It was a propane tank explosion."

"It sounded like a bomb going off. I figured Elvira was back in town." Steve pulled a pack of cigarettes from his pocket and plucked one out. He lit the end and took a big puff before blowing it over Carlita's head.

"Not yet."

They talked for a few more minutes about the upcoming holiday before Steve's next appointment arrived. She told him good-bye, and as soon as they were home, Carlita called Tori. She didn't answer, so she left a message, asking her to return the call at her earliest convenience.

Mercedes drifted into the kitchen and waited for her mother to finish. "Where were you?"

"A better question would be where wasn't I?" Carlita joked. "Let me see. After Detective Wilson cornered me out back, I checked on the pawn shop and noticed the basement trapdoor was open." She told her daughter how she heard an odd *tink* noise and noticed small chunks of brick and mortar piling up.

"Elvira came back," Mercedes guessed.

"Nope. It was Dernice. I went over there to tell her to stop busting down my wall, we found a tunnel and another trapdoor."

"Where did it lead?"

"To an empty building with a perfectly functioning alarm system."

Mercedes grinned as her mother recounted how the alarm went off, Dernice shoved her out of the way and tore down the makeshift ladder. "It was every man for himself, or in this case, every woman for herself."

"At least you know where you stand." Mercedes changed the subject. "Have you had any luck figuring out who owns the other properties on Tybee Island?"

"As a matter of fact, Tori is one of the owners."

"Seriously?" Mercedes' eyes grew round as saucers. "You don't think she has anything to do with the woman's death, do you?"

"No, but she owns property on Tybee. Ten bucks says she knows who owns Savannah's Beach." As if on cue, Carlita's cell phone began to ring. "There she is now."

Carlita tapped the screen and put the call on speaker. "Hi, Tori. Thanks for returning my call. I need your help and wondered if you had time for a quick chat."

"Of course. I always have time for you. Your call sounded urgent."

"Urgent, as in I'm a suspect in the death of a real estate agent for Coastal Adventures."

There was a brief silence on the other end. "Are you serious?"

"Unfortunately. Dernice, Elvira's sister, and I stopped by Coastal's sales office the other day to do a little investigating for Elvira, of all people. I signed

229

the clipboard for more information about the new Coastal Adventures project only hours before the woman was found dead inside Elvira's property."

"Oh, dear. I hadn't heard the details about the woman's death. Well, I may be able to be of some assistance. I haven't seen you in ages. If you're not busy, why don't you come by now? Byron would love to see you, as well."

"I don't want to impose."

"You're not," Tori insisted.

"There's one more thing...I would like to bring someone with me if you don't mind."

"Not Elvira," Tori chuckled.

"Close. Her sister."

"I believe I may have met her, but the memory is vague. Is she anything like Elvira?"

"No, but that doesn't mean she doesn't have quirks of her own," Carlita joked. "We'll be there within the hour." She thanked Tori and ended the call, waving the cell phone in the air. "We may be in luck. Tori may be able to help us with information about the other Tybee property owners."

Chapter 19

Carlita grabbed her keys and swung by Dernice's place to get her before heading out. The trip to the island was slowed by road construction connecting the mainland to the island.

"Looks like they're already gearing up for the big development," Dernice said as they stopped to wait for a front-end loader to move out of the way.

"You should see Coastal's place in St. Augustine. It's a huge complex with an amusement park, shops and restaurants. There's also a bunch of brand-new townhomes for sale." Carlita steered around the loader and gave Dernice a sideways glance. "You mentioned before that you had no idea Elvira was purchasing real estate."

"Not until I opened the mail and found the deed," Dernice sighed heavily.

"That was a heavy sigh."

"I don't know about my sister sometimes. She gets harebrained ideas and doesn't stop to think them through."

They reached Montgomery Hall, a virtual fortress with an electronic gate and call box. A large body of water surrounded the property. It reminded Carlita of a moat, offering Tori both privacy and protection.

Carlita rolled the window down. She pressed the call box button and waited for the beep. "Carlita Garlucci and guest to see Tori."

There was a muffled sound on the other end, and the gate silently opened. "Thank you, Wentworth," Carlita said.

"You're welcome, Mrs. Garlucci."

Dernice eyed her with interest. "You're on a first-name basis with Montgomery's staff?"

"I am."

Dernice gazed out the passenger side window. "I forgot how large this place was. It reminds me of a ritzy country club."

"You've been here before."

"Yeah, right after I got into town and started working with Elvira. We handled the security for a big Christmas shindig."

"It was the Merry Masquerade party. I forgot all about it. It was a great party."

The paved drive leading to the house was long and winding. A canopy of towering oaks, dripping with moss, lined both sides.

Carlita circled the drive and parked in front of the courtyard's massive arched wooden doors.

Dernice unbuckled her seatbelt. "I wonder how much it cost to build this place."

"I have no idea and don't you dare ask Tori," Carlita warned. "It's none of our business."

The courtyard doors slowly opened. Byron, Tori's right-hand man, and someone Carlita considered another close friend, emerged. He approached the driver's side door and held it while she grabbed her purse.

She exited the car and gave him a warm hug. "How are you, Byron? It seems as if the only time I see you anymore is when I've managed to get myself involved in some sort of crisis."

"I am well, Mrs. Garlucci. It's good to see you. Mrs. Montgomery is looking forward to your visit."

Dernice joined them. "Byron Greeley."

"Hello, Dernice."

"You two know each other?"

"We hang out at Big Joe's Pool Hall sometimes. Byron is an ace shooter."

"You're not so bad yourself," Byron complimented. "I haven't seen you around lately."

"I don't have any free time right now. My sister decided to pull a disappearing act. She left me with a big mess."

"Left *us* with a big mess," Carlita interrupted. "Which is why we're here."

"Follow me." Byron plodded ahead, leading the way through the inner courtyard and to the front door.

"These are some swanky digs." Dernice blew air through thinned lips. "You live here, Byron?"

"I do."

The front door opened, and Tori appeared, a wide smile on her face. "Hello, Carlita." She gave Carlita a gentle hug before her sharp blue eyes zeroed in on Dernice.

Carlita watched as she sized the woman up, guessing that she was comparing her to her irritating sibling. "You must be Dernice. I vaguely remember meeting you some time ago."

"I'm easy to forget, unlike my sister." Dernice extended a hand. "Dernice Cobb. Thank you for agreeing to meet with us today."

"You're welcome. Please. Come in." Tori led them into the opulent foyer, past the arched wall cutouts lining the cavernous rotunda.

Dernice paused to admire a work of art. "You have a Zao Wou-Ki piece."

Tori lifted a brow and stared at Dernice. "I do. I just acquired it a few weeks ago. You're familiar with his work?"

"Familiar? He's one of my favorites." Dernice leaned in as she studied the art. "Never seen one of his works in real life before. This is a magnificent piece."

"It is." Tori joined Dernice, and they admired the painting. "In his later years, Wou-Ki was known for his post-war and contemporary art."

Dernice pointed to the silhouettes of two men in the lower left-hand corner. "This is a brush-and-ink technique. Zao was only twenty-one when he presented his first exhibition in Chongqing."

Tori slowly nodded. "His formative years were largely influenced by Western modernism and the work of the Impressionists and Expressionists. It was after his move to Paris that his paintings began to shift toward abstraction."

"He's been dead almost a decade now." Dernice sucked in a breath. "What I wouldn't give to have been able to pick his brain before he died."

"Are you sure you're related to Elvira?" Tori joked.

"Elvira dabbles in art too," Carlita said. "Remember the time she set her apartment on fire, working on a creation?"

"I don't recall hearing that story," Tori said.

"It was a bust, and she was using a blowtorch. She set the curtains on fire."

"I remember you mentioned Elvira setting her apartment on fire, but I didn't hear the part where she used a blowtorch," Dernice snorted. "That was dumb."

"And so was using it inside an apartment building, next to a set of curtains. It was the last straw. I evicted her."

"Gotta love my sister. My life is complete now that I've actually seen a work by Zao." Dernice shoved her hands in her pockets and rocked back on her heels. "If you don't mind me asking, how much did this piece set you back?"

"Set me back?"

"How much did it cost," Dernice clarified.

"Dernice," Carlita gasped. "Your question is crass and rude."

"It's all right." Tori waved dismissively. "I purchased this particular piece for seventy-five thousand dollars."

"Whoa." Dernice made a choking sound and pressed a hand to her throat.

"Some have cost more. Some have cost substantially less."

"You have more pieces?"

Carlita thought Dernice was going to pass out.

"As a matter of fact, I do." Tori resumed her pace and continued down the hall to the study.

Byron was waiting for them at the end and held the door. "Would you like tea service?"

Tori shifted to the side, waiting for her guests to enter the room. "Do you have time to stay for tea?"

"I can," Dernice answered. "Heck, I would move in here if I could, although I don't know where I would park my Harley."

"Harley?"

"My motorcycle."

Tori burst out laughing. "You are most certainly an intriguing woman."

"I'll take that as a compliment." Dernice squared her shoulders. "I like to pride myself on being learned enough for any situation."

"Tea, it is." Byron backed out of the room.

"Let's sit by the fireplace."

Dernice and Carlita took the chairs on one side while Tori eased into the one opposite them. "You said you were a suspect in Kim Turbell's death."

"I am." Carlita briefly told her friend how she, along with Dernice, had visited Tybee Island. "Later that day, the woman from Coastal Adventure's sales office was found dead inside Elvira's building."

"I don't see how this would make you a suspect," Tori said.

"Because I put my name on a signup sheet to get more information about Coastal's project, only hours before Turbell's death."

"Still not enough for you to be a suspect."

Dernice spoke. "Except the reason we were on the island was to check out Elvira's property, which is where the woman's body was found."

"That could present a problem."

"Not to mention Elvira and I are neighbors," Carlita pointed out.

Tori rested her chin on her hand. "What does Elvira say about all of this?"

"She's in St. Augustine, Florida, sorting out a mess of her own," Dernice answered. "Because my sister has been vague on the details, Carlita and I have been trying to piece a few things together. My sister was handling the security for some of the area businesses a few months back, including for Coastal. She knew Atlantic Deep was planning a big project and was in the process of purchasing area properties. She bought one of the properties, my guess is for pennies on the dollar, planning to sell it to them and make a huge profit."

"You are correct," Tori confirmed. "Coastal is buying up the properties. There are four left they need to acquire to move forward with their project. Mine is one, Elvira's is another."

"Right, but there's a small glitch," Carlita said.

"Glitch?"

"Elvira's husband is part-owner of Atlantic Deep, the company behind Coastal Adventure's project."

Tori's jaw dropped. "Her husband?"

"She thought they were divorced." Dernice waved her hand. "It's a big mess. She thought the divorce was final years ago and only recently found out there was a small snafu. Technically, she's still married."

Tori pressed the tips of her fingers together. "She buys this property, thinking she's going to make a killing on it. She discovers her not-an-ex-husband is part owner and won't sell because..."

"He's hired a lawyer and is interested in Elvira's assets," Carlita answered.

"I wondered why she was holding up the sales. I can tell you the other sellers are not very happy with her. Coastal has offered an attractive price to each of us. I figured she would be the first in line to jump on the offer."

"She's using the property as leverage against her husband. If she sells the property and she can't get the divorce finalized, he could take half of her properties or assets."

"Perhaps she killed the woman," Tori said.

"She's in St. Augustine."

Tori started to reply when Byron returned, carrying a silver tray. Mrs. O'Brien, Tori's cook, waddled in behind him, pushing a cart laden with tiered trays of tasty treats.

She gave Carlita a quick smile. "Mrs. Garlucci. It's so good to see you again."

"Hello, Mrs. O'Brien. It's nice to see you too."

"When Mrs. Montgomery told me you were stopping by for a visit, I said to myself, 'Mary, we need to fix something special for Carlita and her guest.'" Mrs. O'Brien slid the cart in next to the coffee table.

After she finished, Byron placed the silver tray with a teapot and teacups on the coffee table.

"Is this Tea Forte?" Tori asked.

"It is. Dolce Vita – honeyed pear."

"Perfect."

Mrs. O'Brien moved the tray of goodies to the center of the coffee table, giving the trio easy access. "My savory cheese scones are filled with thin slices of apple and chutney. The scones are the perfect accompaniment to the tea. There are also a fresh batch of raspberry and dark chocolate teacakes along with ham and roast beef sandwiches."

"I can't wait to dig in." Dernice rubbed her hands together, hungrily eyeing the treats.

Tori caught Carlita's eye and winked. "Well, you had best dig in." She handed Dernice a small plate.

Carlita sucked in a breath, waiting for her to grab one with her hands. Instead, she reached for the tongs and delicately selected one of the sandwiches. She added a cheese scone and then passed the tongs to Carlita.

While they ate, the conversation returned to Coastal Adventure's project.

"Are you involved in Elvira's new investment company?" Tori asked.

Dernice nibbled the edge of her scone. "I had no idea she even started it until the Warranty Deed showed up in the mail."

"So, you're not a part of her get-rich-quick-with-real-estate scheme," Tori said.

"Nope. Carlita and I think the recent incidents – someone forcing my van off the road and the dead woman are somehow related to the sale of the remaining properties and their owners."

"I think it's her husband," Carlita sipped her tea. "He has motive and opportunity."

"Did he...the husband...know the dead woman? Obviously, the answer would be yes since she was an employee of his company."

"I'm sure he did," Carlita said. "Are you concerned about the big development coming to Tybee?"

"I'm both concerned and saddened." Tori told them she and her husband had owned the property for many years. "Of course, we never had big plans for it. We always hoped Tybee would remain a small beach town."

"Is there any way to stop Coastal?" Dernice asked.

"No, short of a miracle. My belief is if we don't willingly sell, they'll somehow force our hands. I'm too old for that kind of fight."

"Can they do that?"

"They have their ways." Tori sampled one of the sandwiches and reached for a raspberry and dark chocolate teacake. "Unfortunately, it is only a matter of time."

Carlita finished the rest of her tea. She set the cup on the saucer and carefully placed both on top of the silver tray. "The reason I called you was to see if you know the identity of the fourth property owner. You are one. Elvira is the second. Ken Gibbons is the third. We haven't been able to figure out who's behind Savannah's Beach. The property is in a trust, meaning we're having difficulty tracking down the owner."

"We figured you, having all of the island connections, would know who it is." Dernice inched forward in her chair.

"As a matter of fact, I do know who owns it." Tori rattled off the owner's name, and Carlita's jaw dropped.

Chapter 20

"Mayor Clarence Puckett." Carlita blinked rapidly. "Savannah's mayor owns the last parcel of property?"

"Correct." Tori nodded.

"This puts a whole new spin on things."

"Which is why I said I believe it's only a matter of time before Atlantic Deep purchases the remaining four properties they need to move forward, including Elvira's. Puckett will see to it."

Carlita grew quiet, her head spinning as she attempted to digest the information. "Do you think the mayor could be responsible for the woman's death?"

"I don't know Mr. Puckett well. He would have no reason to harm Kim Turbell. At least not that I'm aware of, although we all knew Ms. Turbell. She was handling both sides, negotiating the purchase of the properties as well as eventually overseeing the selling of the investment units once the project was finished. As you said, Elvira is the only holdout. If you recall, Mayor Puckett was related – cousins I think – to that dreadful man who was involved in human trafficking a year or so ago."

"Lawson Bates." Lawson Bates had owned a riverboat, the Mystic Dream. When Pirate Pete, who was also Bates' competition, was being investigated for a horrific attack of a local businessman, Carlita had done some digging around. She even went so far as to go along with Mercedes sneaking onto his riverboat one night where they stumbled upon a group of illegal immigrants who were living onboard.

It turned out Bates was involved in human trafficking and used his boat to ferry the poor victims from southern islands, north and to points inland to sell them.

"You know the saying," Dernice said, "the apple doesn't fall far from the tree. Maybe the whole family is corrupt."

"And you know what they say about politicians," Carlita added. "I guess this means we need to do some more digging around. I did think of something. The other day Mercedes and I visited a shop on Tybee. The owner was adamant that she had no plans to sell."

"Was it Tippy Zilman?"

"I don't know her name," Carlita said. "It was a small gift shop."

"I'm sure you're talking about Tippy's place. She's been there for years. She won't sell, but then Coastal doesn't need her property to move forward, at least not yet." Tori finished her tea and glanced at the clock on the fireplace mantle. "I almost forgot. I have a conference call in ten minutes." She stood, her sign that the meeting was over. "Ken Gibbons is the fourth owner. He owns Sunrise Bar and Grill."

"A restaurant owner?"

"Yes. The restaurant is here on Tybee."

Carlita thanked Tori for meeting them on such short notice, for the tea and treats, and for the information while Dernice lingered behind to admire the Zao artwork. "Do you mind if I take a picture of this?"

"Of course not." Tori smiled indulgently. "Perhaps when I have more time, you can come back for another visit, and I'll show you some of my other pieces. It's refreshing to talk art with someone knowledgeable."

Dernice's eyes lit. "I would love to do that. Let me know when."

Tori promised she would be in touch before escorting them to the courtyard and returning inside.

"Victoria Montgomery is one cool cat." Dernice walked at a fast clip. Carlita hurried to keep up as they crossed the courtyard. "I wonder why she and Elvira didn't hit it off."

"Because Elvira trespassed, and Tori had her arrested. That's one of the reasons. Besides, your sister lacks polished social skills."

The women were silent as they made the return trip to the main road. Finally, Carlita, who was mulling over everything Tori had told them, spoke. "We basically have one suspect, Elvira's ex...er, husband."

"I dunno," Dernice shrugged. "I haven't seen Gremlin in years, but he never struck me as the killer-type. I think we still need to take a closer look at Ken Gibbons, the restaurant owner, and Mayor Puckett. What about Mrs. Montgomery?"

"Tori isn't responsible. Besides, we don't even know the woman's cause of death yet."

"I have a connection. Maybe I can find out." Dernice retrieved her cell phone from the center console. She tapped the screen and held the phone to her ear. "Hey. It's Dernice. I need a little intel. I'm trying to figure out the cause of death of a real estate agent yesterday on Tybee Island."

There was a moment of silence. "Kim Turbell. Yeah. That's her. What's the four-one-one?"

"Strangulation. What a terrible way to go. Okay. Thanks." Dernice started to end the call. "What? No kidding. That's weird." She thanked the person on the other end again and dropped the phone back in the console. "Kim Turbell was strangled. Whoever did her in left her purse untouched with cash and credit cards inside, along with some jewelry she was wearing. Nothing was taken."

"Robbery wasn't the motive."

"Nope."

Carlita consulted the clock on the dashboard. It was getting late. "I had hoped we could swing back by the properties, but I don't have time today. My evening is booked."

"Hot date?" Dernice teased.

Carlita shot her an annoyed look. "It's a business meeting with one of my partners."

"Pete Taylor."

"How do you know?"

"Elvira told me he had the hots for you. She noticed it at your son's wedding. In fact, she and I have a bet on how long it will take before you two get hitched."

"You have not," Carlita gasped.

Dernice tugged on her seatbelt. "I say by next year. Elvira thinks you'll get engaged and then break the engagement when you get cold feet."

"Neither one of you will win."

"We'll see," Dernice grinned. "In the meantime, I'm pretty confident my hundred bucks is going to double. You're a solid person and not one to toy with a person's emotions."

Thankfully, they reached the parking lot, and the conversation about Carlita's love life ended.

Dernice waited for her in the alley. "What time do you want to head to Tybee Island to start digging around for more clues?"

"How does late morning sound? That way, we can avoid the morning rush hour traffic."

"Sounds good. Enjoy your date." Dernice winked and then sauntered off, whistling as she walked away.

Carlita briefly closed her eyes as she watched her slip inside her building. "I can't believe those two."

*****

Carlita had enough time for a quick shower, to change into a pair of slacks and a light sweater, fluff her hair and spritz some perfume on. While she scrambled around getting ready, Pete called to remind her to wear comfortable shoes and to bring a jacket.

He arrived promptly at five-thirty and rang the outer bell. She paused long enough to give herself a final once over before dashing down the stairs to let him in.

She peeked through the peephole before flipping the deadbolt and swinging the door open. "You're right on time."

"Aye. Can't keep my favorite lass waiting, now can I?" Pete shifted his arm from behind his back and produced a bouquet of pink roses. "These are for you."

"For me?" Carlita gave the bouquet, dotted with sprigs of baby's breath, a twirl as she admired the flowers. A pink satin bow was tied around the bottom. "Thank you. They're beautiful."

"You're welcome. I picked the prettiest ones I could find to give them to the prettiest gal I know."

Carlita's cheeks turned a tinge of pink at the compliment. "Let's run upstairs so I can put them in water."

Mercedes heard them in the kitchen and wandered out of her room. "Those are beautiful flowers, Pete."

"Aren't they?" Carlita made quick work of retrieving a glass vase. She filled it with water and carefully eased the roses inside. She swapped out the dining room centerpiece and placed the vase in the center before standing back to admire them. "I can't remember the last time someone brought me flowers. I want to take a picture."

Carlita grabbed her cell phone off the counter.

Mercedes reached for her mother's phone. "Let me take a picture of you and Pete with the roses."

Pete moved in next to Carlita and placed a light arm around her shoulder. Her pulse kicked up a notch as she felt the warmth of his hand on her arm. He moved in even closer, and her heart went from pitter-patter to hammering in her chest. It was so loud, she was certain he could hear it.

Mercedes snapped a couple pictures of the smiling couple before handing the phone to her mother. "Should I wait up?" she teased.

"Aren't you and Sam going out tonight?" Saturday night was date night for Mercedes and Sam, typically consisting of an evening spent in the popular and touristy City Market district, only a few short blocks from Walton Square.

"No. He's booked for a special tour tonight. We're gonna go out tomorrow night instead."

"It must be important for him to book an evening tour on date night."

"I guess so. He wouldn't tell me anything about it. He said he was sworn to secrecy." Mercedes leaned her hip against the counter. "Autumn and I are going to the movies. There's a new chick flick we want to see."

Pete helped Carlita slip her jacket on. "Tis a nice night for an evening out."

"Have fun." Mercedes followed them to the door, and after they left, quietly closed it behind them.

"Where are we going now?" Carlita asked.

"To the alley."

"The alley?"

"You'll see."

Pete held the door and offered his hand as he helped Carlita step off the stoop. The couple made small talk about the weather, Pete's pirate ship venture, and area restaurants that had recently opened. All the while in the back of her mind, she wondered why they hadn't left yet.

The back door to the apartment eased open. Sam Ivey emerged, looking dapper dressed in his striped seersucker suit. He coaxed Sadie, his pup, out behind him. "Hello, Carlita, Pete."

"Good evening, Sam." A mischievous grin spread across Pete's face.

"It's the perfect weather for an evening tour." Sam placed his signature straw hat on top of his head and gave it a light tap.

"Yes, it is. We were just agreeing what a beautiful evening it is." Carlita bent down to pat Sadie's head. "Sam and Sadie's Savannah Tours in action. Mercedes told us you had a very important tour this evening."

"I do. Sadie and I are raring to go."

Pete winked at Sam and extended his arm to Carlita. "Well...shall we get on with our date?"

"I'm ready." Carlita slipped her arm in Pete's arm, and the trio began walking down the alley. She shot her tenant a puzzled glance. "We're going in the same direction?"

"I believe we are," Sam said.

They reached the stop sign at the corner, waiting for a car to pass before continuing to the next block. The more they walked, the more confused Carlita became. "You still haven't told me where we're going."

"On a tour," Pete explained. "We're going on a tour of Historic Savannah."

Carlita abruptly stopped, her eyes narrowing. "You. Sam is our surprise date!"

The smile on Pete's face widened. "Yes. You once told me you had never taken a proper tour of our lovely city. I thought it was a great idea for our first official date, and I managed to hire the best tour guide in Savannah."

"I can't disagree with you there," Carlita said. "Well, then. Carry on, Sam and Sadie. I can't wait to find out more about my home."

Chapter 21

We'll start our tour in the Riverfront District at the city's most famous hotel."

"The Marshall House," Pete guessed.

"Correct. Marshall House was built in the eighteen hundreds. It was once used as a hospital for Union soldiers and twice during the yellow fever epidemic."

They slowed when they reached the exterior of the four-story hotel. Sam set Sadie on the sidewalk, and she began to explore as far as her leash would allow.

While Sadie scoped out her surroundings, Sam explained that the hotel underwent extensive renovations in the late nineties, with great efforts taken to ensure the hallmarks of the historic hotel were preserved.

"Those that couldn't be preserved were painstakingly recreated. We aren't going in, but when you get a chance, it's worth taking the time to check out the inside. Many of the wood floors are the original hardwoods, along with wood-burning fireplaces, exterior brick walls, and several clawfoot tubs dating back to eighteen eighty."

"It's beautiful." Carlita peered up at the iron veranda.

They finished walking along the Riverfront District, stopping when they reached the Congregation Mickve Israel.

"This is the third oldest Jewish synagogue in the United States. The synagogue contains a 15th Century Torah, the first five books of the Bible, and is the oldest Torah in North America. The synagogue also houses a collection of letters from George Washington, Thomas Jefferson, James Madison and several other presidents."

"Fascinating," Carlita murmured. "I didn't realize I knew so little about Savannah's history."

"It would take weeks to give you a tour of the entire city. I learn new information all of the time, sometimes from my guests."

They cut through the City Market, making their way to the other end of the bustling square.

"At one time, there were twenty-four squares, but now there are only twenty-two. The most famous are the ones with the fountains. The *Forrest Gump* movie put Savannah on the map, as well as the book, *Midnight in the Garden of Good and Evil*." Sam told them he highly recommended both.

By the time they finished the tour, Carlita's head was spinning with information, and she had a greater appreciation for the uniqueness and history of her adopted home.

Sam escorted them to their starting point, the alley behind the apartment. Sadie let out a low whine and flopped down on the ground. "Sadie is tuckered out. It's time for us to head home."

"Thank you for a wonderful tour," Carlita lightly touched his arm. "It was the perfect way to spend the evening."

"I couldn't agree more," Pete chimed in. "And now I owe you and Mercedes an evening cruise and dinner on board The Flying Gunner."

"We'll be taking you up on that soon. Enjoy the rest of your evening." Sam tipped his hat before scooping up his pup and returning inside.

Pete waited for the door to close behind them before reaching for Carlita's hand. "All of our walking and touring has left me famished. The first half of our date is over, so now begins our second half. I'm leaving this part up to you. Where would you like to dine?"

"I..." There were so many wonderful restaurants in the area she was itching to try, but there was one in particular she was anxious to visit – the one on Tybee Island owned by Ken Gibbons. "Do you mind taking a drive to Tybee? I want to check out a restaurant...bar and grill something."

"Sunrise Bar and Grill. Their ocean view is spectacular, and the seafood is very good." Pete extended his arm, and they leisurely strolled to the end of the block before crossing the street. Pete's Parrot House Restaurant was a few short feet away.

He told Carlita to wait on the porch while he went to get his vehicle. He pulled up moments later behind the wheel of a shiny blue Ford pickup truck. He left the engine idling and circled around the front. "Shall we?"

"I didn't know you owned a pickup truck." Carlita grabbed the handle with one hand as she hoisted herself onto the running board and scooted across the seat.

"There's a lot of things you don't know about me," Pete teased. "Perhaps we should spend more time together."

Butterflies sent her stomach fluttering as she waited for Pete to shut her door.

He returned to the other side, easily swinging into the driver's seat. "The truck comes in handy for hauling equipment and supplies from the restaurant to the ship and back. I've decided it's time to put my house up for sale and move into the apartment I've been renovating above the Parrot House."

Pete explained that he'd owned his ranch home and several acres of land on the outskirts of town for years. He realized he spent wasted hours running back and forth between his businesses. "I spend half my nights sleeping on the ship and figured maybe it was time to sell my place and move to town."

"I don't blame you."

"Annie Dowton has agreed to list it for me. She's a real gem."

"Yes, she is," Carlita agreed. "If I'm ever in the market for more property, I'll call Annie."

Pete cast her a sideways glance. "So, why the sudden interest in Sunrise Bar and Grill?"

"Death," Carlita said bluntly. "A real estate agent for Coastal Adventures, a company purchasing properties for a new Tybee Island venture, was found dead inside Elvira's Tybee Island property. Her property also happens to be one the company is trying to purchase."

"Elvira's got her hands in everything," Pete said.

"Yes, and she doesn't even have to be here to cause chaos."

"What does the woman's death and Sunrise have to do with you?"

"Dernice and I stopped by the sales office only hours before the woman's death. While I was there, I put my name and contact information on the sign-up sheet, inquiring about properties." Carlita explained that after filling it out, they visited Elvira's property to have a look around.

"And her body was found inside Elvira's building."

"Yes. Savannah Detective Skip Wilson has already questioned me. He knows I drove to St. Augustine to meet with Elvira. He also knows that I met Coastal Adventures' sales agent just hours before her death."

"And Ken Gibbons, the owner of Sunrise, is somehow involved?"

"He owns a piece of property Atlantic Deep is anxious to purchase for Coastal Adventure's project." Carlita lifted a brow. "You know Gibbons?"

"As a matter of fact, I do," Pete said. "Savannah, not to mention Tybee Island, are small communities. We both own restaurants and have known each other for years, ever since Ken took over running the restaurant."

Carlita grew silent as she processed the information. Pete was right. Savannah and Tybee Island were small communities.

"I'm surprised you haven't heard his name before." Pete stopped at the light. He waited for it to turn green before turning left and toward the water.

They drove along Tybee Island's main drag to the end of the street before pulling into an empty parking spot near the corner of a tall blue building. "This is it."

Carlita reached for the door handle. Pete stopped her. "I'll come around to open your door." She gazed into his gray-green eyes, and her stomach did a flip-flop.

"My goal is to make this date so memorable you won't hesitate to accept when I ask again," he said softly.

"You're on the right track."

Her eyes followed him as he walked around the front of the truck to the passenger side. Pete opened the door and helped her down.

"Thank you. It's higher up than it looks."

"It is." Pete placed a light hand on the center of her back and guided her down the narrow sidewalk.

Carriage lights lined the sidewalks, illuminating the walkway and beckoning them inside. The clapboard façade was faded, and the building's exterior reminded Carlita of a warehouse.

They crossed the front porch and stepped inside. A bar, filled with patrons, ran along the left-hand side. Several large screen televisions blared loudly.

A young woman approached the hostess station. "Good evening. Table for two?"

"Yes, and a quiet one if you have it," Pete said.

The woman consulted her seating chart. "I have the perfect spot." She led them along the bar, through the main dining area and to a second, smaller room. She stopped when they reached the front of the restaurant and a cozy corner overlooking the water. "Will this do?"

"It's perfect." Pete pulled out Carlita's chair and waited for her to have a seat before taking the one next to her. The young woman placed menus on the table. "Your server will be along shortly."

"Thank you." Carlita smiled at her and waited until she was gone. "This is perfect. I love the view." Several small sailboats dotted the water, their lights casting a romantic glow.

"Aye. It's a pretty one."

The server approached and introduced himself before taking their drink order. Carlita splurged on raspberry lemonade, and Pete did the same. While they waited for their drinks, they perused the menu. It had been hours since Carlita had eaten, and everything sounded delicious.

"Let's start with an appetizer," Pete suggested.

"I can't decide. You pick."

Pete chose the crispy shrimp lettuce wraps and placed the order when their drinks arrived. He leaned back, giving the server room to place his drink on the table. "Is Ken in tonight?"

"The owner, Ken Gibbons?"

"Yes."

"He is. He's in the kitchen."

"Could you tell him Pete Taylor and Carlita Garlucci, the owner of Ravello's Italian Eatery, are here?"

"I sure will. I'm heading back there to give the kitchen your appetizer order."

Pete thanked him and waited until he stepped away to check on another table. "I figured you might want to meet Ken. More than likely, you'll cross paths somewhere down the road."

"I'm sure we will."

Pete lifted his glass. "Here's to the first of many enjoyable evenings together."

Carlita lifted her lemonade. "To many more." She sampled her fruity drink. "This is delicious."

"I don't believe I've ever seen you drink anything other than soda or tea."

"I normally don't, but lemonade sounded refreshing." Carlita and Pete discussed business, Luigi's arrival and Pete's upcoming pirate ship event, the one he'd hired Luigi to help with.

"How's it going with Luigi?"

"Okay. I'm not sure if Savannah is a good fit for him. It's a little tame for his lifestyle."

"Has he complained?"

"No, although he strikes me as..." Carlita paused as she searched for the right words. "Perhaps a little restless."

"Not enough action," Pete clarified.

"Something like that."

"And you're concerned if there's not enough action, he may end up creating his own to liven things up."

"The thought has crossed my mind," she admitted.

The appetizer arrived promptly. Carlita slid a wrap onto her plate and sampled a corner of the spicy dish before deeming it perfect. She polished hers off while Pete was still working on his first. "I'm inhaling my food."

"I can appreciate a woman with a hearty appetite," Pete teased.

The server returned a short time later to clear the table and take their dinner order. "I'll get your order right in." He grabbed the menus and retreated, passing by a burly man who was headed in their direction.

"Pete Taylor." The man's booming voice filled the small room.

Pete shoved his chair back and stood. "Ken. It's good to see you again." He grasped the man's arm as they shook hands.

"I stopped by your restaurant last week, but you weren't around."

"I'm sorry I missed you." Pete motioned to Carlita, who was still seated. "I would like you to meet Carlita Garlucci. She owns Ravello's Italian Eatery in Savannah's Walton Square. Carlita, this is Ken Gibbons, the owner of this fine establishment."

Ken shook her hand. Not realizing the strength of his grip, he squeezed hard, and a sharp pain shot down her arm. She forced herself not to wince and let out a sigh of relief when he finally let go. "I was in there a few days ago with my son and had a delicious Italian dish. I think the name was cake-e-o-pep."

"Cacio e pepe," Carlita said. "It means cheese and pepper. It has the taste of a stripped-down macaroni and cheese."

"With a side of steamed mussels." Ken patted his stomach as he smacked his lips. "I'm still thinking about it."

"I'm glad you enjoyed your meal."

The men began talking shop, and Carlita could sense Gibbons' eyes on her. Every time she looked his way, Ken would look away. Finally, the conversation ended when Ken glanced at his watch. "I need to head back to the kitchen. I want to personally oversee the preparation of your meal. I'll stop back by before you leave." He gave them a nod and limped out of the dining room.

"He seems like a...nice man," Carlita said.

"Ken's a great guy. After a few minutes, his loud voice will get your ears to ringing. He lost part of his hearing during his tour in Iraq."

"He's a veteran?" Carlita asked.

"Two tours of duty, which is the reason for his limp. He was injured and returned to the States to take over the family business."

"I'll be sure to thank him for his service."

The food came out a short time later, and Carlita enjoyed every bite of her mahi. Pete and she shared samples, each declaring theirs to be the best.

The server stopped by as they were finishing up and removed the plates. Reluctant for the date to end, Pete ordered decaf coffee, and the conversation turned to the upcoming Thanksgiving holiday. Carlita had already invited Pete to dinner, and he'd accepted her invitation.

The bill arrived, and after Pete paid, Ken was the one to deliver the receipt. "How was dinner?"

"Delicious," Carlita said. "Pete tells me you're a veteran. Thank you for your service."

"You're welcome," Ken said. "It's good to be home."

After he left, Carlita grabbed her purse and joined Pete, who led the way out of the restaurant. They were halfway through the main dining room when she caught the eye of a woman who looked all too familiar.

She did a double-take when she realized who was seated at a table not far from the front door.

Chapter 22

Carlita marched across the dining room to the table for one. "Elvira Cobb."

"What are you doing here?" A look of surprise crossed Elvira's face.

"What am *I* doing here? What are *you* doing here?"

Elvira shrank down in her chair. "Can you lower your voice?"

Carlita temporarily forgot all about Pete and their date. She plopped down in the chair next to Elvira and leaned in. "Have you wrapped up your ex crisis?"

"I'm close."

"Are you meeting with Gibbons to discuss the property sale?"

"It's none of your business. Besides, you're not my keeper."

"Thank the Good Lord. I would go insane trying to keep track of you."

Elvira ignored the jab. "I would ask you the same thing. What are you doing here?"

"Having dinner with Pete." Carlita realized he was standing directly behind her. "We were having a very nice evening until now."

"You're the one who came over. It's not like I was trying to spy on you. I'm here to see my friend, Ken."

"And I'm not spying on you," Carlita hissed. "Listen. Detective Wilson is breathing down my neck. He was on my doorstep earlier today, asking me about Turbell, and then he wanted to know where I had been."

"I told him you visited me in St. Augustine," Elvira said.

"At least we corroborated our stories on that."

"Honesty is the best policy. For the most part." Elvira folded her hands and leaned back in the chair. "I told him the reason you visited me in St. Augustine was because we're partners in a business venture."

"You told him what?" Carlita roared. "You just put an even bigger target on my back." Resisting the urge to shake some sense into the woman, she abruptly stood. "I will not allow you to ruin my wonderful evening. You are your own worst enemy and from here on out, you're on your own."

Pete placed a light hand on her shoulder and gently pulled her away. "It's not worth the aggravation, lass."

Elvira sprang from her chair. "Like it or not, we're in this together. I thought you wanted to help me," she whined. "Besides, you're in just as deep as me, us being partners and all."

"We are not partners," Carlita snapped. "I was happy minding my own business. In fact, we even had a few drama-free weeks while you were gone."

"You miss me. Admit it. Savannah is dull and boring without Elvira Cobb." Elvira lowered her voice. "I think I'm getting close to figuring out who's responsible for the woman's death. That's why I'm here."

Carlita's eyes narrowed. "Does your friend, Ken, know something?"

"Maybe. I don't know yet. I just got here and was waiting for him to meet with me when you decided to make a scene."

"Pete is right. This isn't a conversation worth having. Good luck with your investigation."

"You aren't giving up," Elvira called out after her. "You're in too deep."

Carlita didn't bother answering, didn't bother turning around. Pete helped her back into the truck and then slid behind the wheel. "She's quite adept at getting under your skin."

"No kidding," Carlita muttered as she reached for her seatbelt. "I think she does it on purpose."

"You may be right." Pete steered the conversation to a more pleasant topic, and despite her run-in with Elvira he was able to distract her. The evening ended the way it began – as one of the most pleasant nights she'd had in a very long time.

Pete left the truck running as he made his way to the passenger side and escorted her to the door. He silently gazed at her, his expression unreadable.

Carlita thought he was going to turn to go when he bent down and tenderly kissed her lips. Her breath caught in her throat as the kiss deepened.

Finally, Pete reluctantly lifted his head. "I'm sorry."

"For what?" Carlita asked breathlessly.

"For taking the liberty of kissing you without asking."

"I'm not sorry," Carlita whispered. "It was the perfect ending to a perfect date. Thank you for inviting me and for not giving up on me."

"Giving up on you? Not by a long shot. I guess it would be safe to say if I ask you for a second date, you would be inclined to accept?"

"Definitely inclined," Carlita said. "This is the best evening I have had in a very long time."

"I couldn't agree more. In fact, I'll start planning our next date as soon as I return home." Pete gave her a quick peck on the lips and then returned to his truck. He waved good-bye and then waited for Carlita to make her way into the building.

She stood inside, watching his taillights disappear before floating up the stairs.

The apartment was dark except for the glow of the table lamp near the door.

"Mercedes?" Carlita placed her purse on the barstool. There was no answer. She pulled her cell phone from her purse and set it on the counter when she realized there was a text and a missed call.

The text was from Mercedes, telling her mother that she and Autumn would be home before eleven.

The second was a message from Dernice. "Hey, Carlita. It's Dernice. I'm sorry to bother you during your hot date with the hunky pirate, but I wanted to let you know I heard from Elvira. She said she had some new information. She wouldn't tell me what it was, but I have a feeling she's on her way back here. Call me."

The call abruptly ended. Carlita checked the time. It was nine o'clock. Taking a chance Dernice was still up, she dialed her number.

"Carlita," Dernice answered on the first ring. "How was the date?"

"It was wonderful, except for the ending when Pete and I ran into your sister."

"Here?" Dernice asked. "She said she might be on her way back to town."

"She's on Tybee Island, meeting with Ken Gibbons, a restaurant owner. He's on the list as one of the property owners Atlantic Deep is negotiating with."

There was a long silence on the other end of the line.

"Hello?" Carlita asked.

"I'm still here," Dernice said. "I wonder if she plans to spend the night on Tybee or if she's coming home."

"Who knows with Elvira? For all we know, she could be sleeping in her car."

"She didn't take one with her to St. Augustine," Dernice reminded her.

"You're right. Maybe she's staying with her friend, Ken."

"Could be. Anyway, I'm waiting for her to call me back." Dernice explained she'd been doing some digging around on Coastal Adventures and the employee, Kim Turbell. "The press released some details about her background. There was more going on with that chick than just selling real estate."

"Like what?" Carlita asked.

"I think you should check it out for yourself. Coastal was involved in several questionable business transactions, and I think Turbell was a key player."

"So maybe one of the Tybee business owners wasn't responsible for her death. It also means Elvira's ex or almost-ex is looking more and more like the killer."

"I was thinking along the same lines. Google her name and death, and you'll see what I'm talking about."

Carlita promised she would, but first, she wanted to check on Luigi. She returned downstairs and approached the efficiency at the end of the hall. She could hear muffled sounds coming from within. She gave the door a tentative knock.

Luigi appeared in the doorway. "Hey, Mrs. G."

"Hello, Luigi. I thought I would check to see how you're doing."

"Fine." Luigi began cracking his knuckles. "I was just watchin' some clips on YouTube from last year's convention center cooking contest where the women started brawling. It's the gig I'm working Monday."

"I hope it's not too much to handle on your own."

"Too much to handle?" Luigi grinned widely. "I can't wait. A bunch of women attacking each other over food? It's a free freak show – one I'm gonna get paid to watch."

"I'm glad you're looking forward to it."

"You wanna come in?" Luigi shifted to the side.

"I don't want to bother you."

"It's no bother."

"Maybe for a couple of minutes." Carlita followed him into the efficiency. It was tidy, neat as a pin as her mother would say. There was nothing out of place...no dirty dishes in the sink, no clothes strewn about. "You got the place lookin' good."

"A lot better than the last tenant you had in here."

Carlita couldn't agree more. Angelica Reynolds, her former tenant, had been evicted after she became involved in a physical altercation with Brittney, Carlita's daughter-in-law. "I'm not sure who was more of a pain...Elvira or Angelica."

"She almost got snuffed out," Luigi chuckled. "Makes me kinda miss Princess Brittney."

"Are you regretting your decision to move down here?" Carlita asked. "Seems like life in Savannah is a lot slower pace than what you're used to."

"Yeah. I mean. I don't miss the family. I gotta be honest. I miss the action. The casino was always buzzin' with something. I kinda miss Ricco too."

"How is Ricco?"

Ricco DeGrassi was one of Vito Castellini's "bodyguards." He also lived in New Jersey and was assigned to protecting Vito's family and daughter. Although he had visited Savannah several times, she didn't know him as well as she'd come to know Luigi.

"He's doin' good. He ain't real keen on the partner Vito set him up with. She's a real tool."

Carlita arched a brow. "A woman?"

"Roxy Ciccone. I ain't never liked Roxy. She's two-faced. I think Vito uses her as a plant, to keep his men in line."

"I'll be sure to keep my distance if I ever meet her."

"Oh...you'll meet her all right. She's in charge of protecting Brittney. The next time you see Brittney, you'll meet her."

"I can't wait."

Luigi pulled an unlit cigarette from his pocket and began twirling it between his fingers.

"I'll let you go have a smoke." She wandered into the hall, and Luigi followed her out. He slowed when they reached the back door. "Thanks again, Mrs. G. Thanks for giving me a chance."

Carlita smiled. "You're welcome, Luigi. I hope you enjoy living in Savannah for many years. If you give it a chance, it will grow on you."

Luigi reached for the doorknob before turning back. "I've been meanin' to ask...how's it goin' with Elvira and the dead woman?"

"I'm hoping we'll have more information by tomorrow." Carlita told Luigi to let her know if he needed anything and then returned to the apartment.

Mercedes still wasn't back. Carlita knew she wouldn't be able to sleep until she was home. She remembered Dernice telling her to research the real estate agent and Coastal Adventures. She pulled out her desk chair and perched on the edge.

She typed "Kim Turbell death, Georgia," in the search bar. Several results popped up. At first, there was no new information until Carlita began to dig a little deeper. From the snippets she was able to find, Kim Turbell's previous employment history included a stint as a mortgage lender as well as a stockbroker.

After exhausting her search on Turbell, Carlita typed Coastal Adventures in the search bar. Dernice was right. Several Atlantic Deep projects were under federal investigation. The details were vague, only stating the money to fund the projects may have come from questionable sources.

She decided to go back to searching Turbell's background, but this time accessed social media sites. Most of the information was basic, and nothing stood out.

Carlita leaned back in the chair and stared at the screen. Obviously, the woman had high aspirations for her real estate career. Which meant she probably spent a lot of time working the professional circles.

On a whim, Carlita accessed the LinkedIn site and logged onto her free account. She typed in Kim Turbell's name. A description of her background as a real estate agent appeared.

Her heart plummeted when she discovered the woman's contacts/connections were hidden. She was still staring at the screen when Mercedes arrived home.

Carlita shifted in her chair, waiting for her to hang her jacket on the hook near the door. "How was the movie?"

"It was okay. There were a lot of parts they could've done without." Mercedes wrinkled her nose. "It had way too many sappy love scenes."

"What's wrong with romance?" Carlita gave her daughter a pointed stare. "Poor Sam."

"Speaking of Sam and dates, how was your date with Pete?" Mercedes made googly eyes.

"It was wonderful. A perfect date, thanks in part to Sam and Sadie."

"What did Sam have to do with your date?"

"Pete surprised me with a tour of the city. Sam and Sadie were our guides."

"Seriously?" Mercedes kicked her shoes off. "Sam was your surprise?"

"Yes, and he did a wonderful job. I learned a lot about Savannah and its history. You should take a tour too."

"I want to, but I want to do a haunted tour. I'm waiting on Sam to figure out what works best and then coordinate it with some of the other tour guides."

"After the tour, Pete and I visited Tybee Island and had dinner at Sunrise Bar and Grill on the water. The owner is Ken Gibbons."

"Ken Gibbons. The name sounds familiar. Isn't he the owner of one of the properties that Atlantic Deep is trying to purchase?"

"Yes, which is why I chose the place. As luck would have it, Pete and Ken know each other. He was at the restaurant, and came out and introduced himself. He's a nice man, a veteran who was injured in Iraq." Carlita remembered the way he stared at her. "Something about him made me uneasy."

"Uneasy how?"

"The way he stared at me." Carlita shivered. "I dunno. Maybe I'm just being paranoid."

Mercedes wandered across the room. "Did you learn anything new about Coastal Adventures or the island's property owners?"

"No. It was pretty much a bust." Carlita told her daughter how, on the way out, she spotted Elvira in the restaurant. "She was there to meet with Ken."

"Then maybe she should come home."

"I said the same thing. She claims she's close to wrapping up her ex issue."

Mercedes glanced at her mother's computer screen. "You have a LinkedIn account?"

"Yeah. I logged on to try to research Kim Turbell. Unfortunately, I only have a free account, so I can't access her connections. I was hoping maybe if I found out who her connections were, I could see if any of them hit my radar."

"If you sign up for a regular account, you can access her information."

"How much is that gonna cost?"

"I'm not sure." Mercedes squeezed in next to her mother and reached for the mouse. "I think the cheapest plan is thirty bucks a month."

"Thirty bucks a month? Just to research the woman's background?"

"You don't have to do it."

"But I want to know. Fine. Sign me up. If I don't think it's useful, I'll cancel." Carlita blew air through thinned lips as she watched her daughter set up a paid account. She finished entering the information and stood. "You're all set. Snoop away."

"Thanks." Carlita entered Kim Turbell's name in the search bar. Her account appeared again, this time with more information. She scrolled through the woman's connections when one, in particular, caught her eye.

Chapter 23

"I think I found something," Carlita said. "Kim Turbell was friends or was 'linked' to Mayor Puckett."

Not only was Kim connected to Savannah's mayor, but she was also friends with the Tybee Island mayor and several city council members.

Carlita scanned the list of names and noticed there were also local business owners' profiles, including Ken Gibbons.

"There's EC Security Services," Mercedes pointed at the screen.

"Sure enough." Carlita drummed her fingers on the desk. "Elvira failed to mention that little tidbit of information. Perhaps she knew Turbell better than she let on."

"I'm not defending Elvira, but I would think she would want as many local business owners and business contacts as possible to grow her accounts. Maybe Elvira doesn't even realize she's connected to Turbell."

"You're giving Elvira too much credit. I think she does know it and either doesn't think it's an issue or doesn't think anyone will find out."

"So, now what? Turbell has a bunch of connections, including Elvira. I'm sure the investigators are more interested in Elvira than in focusing on you," Mercedes said.

"Except for the fact they questioned her, and she told them I visited her in St. Augustine," Carlita said. "Because we're business partners."

"Business partners?" Mercedes frowned. "Why would she tell them that?"

"Because she thought it would help. The authorities know I visited Elvira, the owner of the Tybee Island where Turbell's body was found, while

I was in St. Augustine, and now Elvira has put the bug in their ear that she and I are business partners."

Carlita ran a ragged hand through her hair. "I'm sure it's only a matter of time before the cops are on my doorstep again. I can eventually prove Elvira is lying, that we aren't partners, but who knows how long it will take."

Mercedes patted her mother's arm. "I would hang tight. Maybe the authorities will figure out who is responsible."

"I hope so." Carlita's expression grew grim as she turned the computer off. "I'm taking Rambo out."

After returning from their short trip to Rambo's grassy strip, Carlita turned in. She tossed and turned all night, wondering how on earth the woman managed to cause so much trouble when she wasn't even around.

She finally fell asleep and woke when Rambo began whining at the door. Carlita stumbled to the kitchen and started a pot of coffee. Her cell phone, which was sitting on the counter, chirped.

Carlita eyed the clock. It was only seven-ten. She snatched the phone off the counter and glanced at the screen. It was Elvira. Cranky from lack of sleep, she answered the call and got right to the point. "What do you want?"

"What kind of greeting is that?"

"The way I answer it when I know it's you," Carlita said rudely. "I barely slept last night, wondering if the cops were going to show up any minute with an arrest warrant."

"You worry too much." Elvira changed the subject. "I have a plan."

"I'm not interested."

"You haven't even heard it."

"I don't need to. I already told you that you were on your own. This whole EC Investment Group, you trying to make a quick buck when you don't know diddly about real estate has come back to bite you. Somehow, I have, once again, managed to get caught in the middle of your shenanigans. At this point, I'm going to suggest Luigi have nothing to do with your company if he wants to stay sane and alive. Leave me out of whatever new disaster you're concocting. End of discussion."

There was silence on the other end of the line, and Carlita knew the wheels were spinning in Elvira's head.

"You're not thinking clearly."

"You're right. I'm not." Carlita tightened her grip on the phone. "I'm exhausted, stressed out and ticked off."

"You really should look into anger management exercises. It's not healthy to get so worked up."

A sudden thought occurred to Carlita; actually, it was brilliant. "I want to buy your building."

"Buy my building? What does this have to do with you being a murder suspect?"

"Everything. I wouldn't be a suspect if it wasn't for you. If you move away, it will eliminate ninety-nine percent of my stresses."

"What about your mafia ties? You can run, but you can't hide from the family, especially when one of your kids is involved with them."

"My family is none of your concern."

"Whatever. My building isn't for sale. I'm in the perfect location."

"For torturing me."

"We need to stop bickering and get back to your current crisis," Elvira said. "The authorities aren't going to stop searching. I have a plan to uncover the killer and whoever has been behind the attacks. I'm almost certain now that my ex is involved. My plan will only take a couple of hours of your time."

Carlita sucked in a breath. The last thing she needed was to continue to be involved in anything Elvira cooked up. Everything the woman touched or was even remotely involved in turned into a disaster.

"I'm also ready to sell. I'll give you a cut of whatever I get out of the Tybee Island property. Ten percent."

"Ten percent of what?" Carlita thought she'd heard a number thrown around but couldn't remember what it was.

"Two hundred fifty thousand. You could make a quick twenty-five thousand for a couple of hours, plus bring a killer to justice, *and* I would return home."

"That's a case for not helping you," Carlita joked.

"Very funny. Well?"

"I..." Carlita slowly wandered to the window and stared at the side of Elvira's building. "Does it involve illegal activities?"

"Nope. There is one stipulation."

"Here we go." Carlita rolled her eyes.

"You have to pretend we're partners."

"Which won't be hard since you've already told everyone, including the cops, that's the case."

"See? It will work out perfectly. The only snag is it would help me if I knew the name of the fourth Tybee property owner."

"I know who it is." Carlita started to tell Elvira and then changed her mind.

"Who is it?" she demanded.

"Why does it matter to you? You plan to have me handle your dirty work." Carlita watched as a Savannah police car turned onto the alley. They drove to the other end and pulled into the parking lot. "The cops are here."

"To see you?" Elvira asked.

"It's either me or Dernice. I have to go."

"Wait! What are you..."

Carlita hung up. Detective Wilson and another man, this one a uniformed officer, exited the vehicle and began circling Elvira's parking lot.

Certain she was probably next on their list, Carlita made a beeline for the bathroom to get ready. While she showered, she wondered what kind of plan Elvira had in mind.

Every time Elvira was involved, it didn't end well. Somehow, there was a link between Tybee Island and the woman's death. Perhaps Kim's death was unrelated to whoever had forced Dernice's van off the road.

She finished showering and threw on a pair of slacks and a button-down blouse. Carlita made her way to her desk and computer. She switched it on and then typed in Mayor Clarence Puckett's name.

A handful of news stories popped up. There was a quote from him about the re-opening of the recently renovated city hall.

He was also quoted singing the praises of Coastal Adventure and the new Tybee Island project, telling the news reporter he thought it was a wonderful opportunity for the island. He failed to mention he had a vested interest in the success of the venture.

Below that was another story, this one about the authorities re-opening the investigation into Puckett's wife's death.

Carlita's heart skipped a beat as she read the story. The mayor's wife, Mariella, had died several years back. Her death was ruled a suicide after her SUV was found partially submerged in the Savannah River. Mariella was still in the vehicle and buckled in the driver's seat.

Puckett had taken out a substantial life insurance policy on Mariella only a few short months before her suicide, and her family had sued to have the case re-opened.

The last paragraph ended with news about Puckett's involvement in Coastal Adventure's project as both a property seller and investor.

Carlita read the story twice. Puckett's wife had died, and he collected on a large life insurance policy. He was now investing in the Coastal Adventure's project and had even touted it as a benefit to the community. No one would benefit more than a man who was financially involved.

Had Kim Turbell found something out about Coastal? About Elvira's ex or even Puckett? The mayor moved up a notch on her list of possible suspects.

Despite Carlita's fear that the cops would be pounding on her door at any moment, it never happened. Thinking she had dodged a bullet and the police weren't after her, she decided it was time to head to the nearby superstore to stock up on Thanksgiving Day dinner supplies. Carlita finished working on her shopping list. Mercedes still hadn't made an appearance, so she left a note on the kitchen counter and headed out.

The store was packed with holiday shoppers, and it took her twice as long as usual to find everything on her list. Returning home, her first stop was the restaurant to drop off the frozen turkeys.

The morning prep crew hadn't arrived yet, so Carlita let herself in the back door and carried them to the walk-in freezer. She taped notes on top to let the staff know the turkeys belonged to her before returning to the car.

It took several trips from the parking lot to the apartment to unload the groceries and even longer for her to make room inside her cupboards and the fridge.

Feeling festive and in the holiday spirit, she'd even purchased a cornucopia centerpiece, a smiling scarecrow and some spice scented fall candles for the fireplace mantle.

Carlita had just finished decorating when someone rapped loudly on the hall door. She eased it open to find a sheepish Sam Ivey standing on the other side.

"Good morning, Sam."

"Hello, Carlita. I'm sorry to bother you so early. Mercedes stopped by last night after the movies and forgot her cell phone. I'm heading out for my first tour. Is she up?"

"Not yet."

"Could you give this to her?" Sam held out Mercedes' phone.

"Of course. I'm surprised she forgot it. She takes this thing everywhere."

"She may have been distracted," Sam teased mischievously.

"I'm sure she was. Thanks again for the awesome tour last night. Pete and I both enjoyed it immensely."

"Where did you end up going for dinner?"

"The Sunrise Bar and Grill on Tybee Island. It was very good."

"I know the owner, Ken Gibbons. He's a vet."

"Yes. I met him. Pete knows him, as well. I heard he was wounded while serving," Carlita said.

"Yeah. Ken came back to take over the family restaurant business a few years ago and had to clean up a few family messes."

"I can certainly sympathize."

"I think he's back on track now and no longer plans to put the restaurant up for sale again."

Carlita perked up. "He was planning on selling his restaurant?"

"I...I shouldn't have said anything. It's none of my business."

"Why would he have to sell the restaurant?"

Sam frowned. "I can't tell you. I'm sorry."

"When you were still a cop, you served him papers in an official capacity." Carlita could tell from the look on Sam's face she was on the right track. "He returned, wounded. Gibbons took over the family business. It was in some sort of trouble that involved money."

Sam shook his head.

"It's okay." Carlita lifted a hand. "I shouldn't have put you on the spot. One of Coastal Adventure's real estate agents was found dead...strangled, inside Elvira's investment property. Atlantic Deep, the owner of Coastal Adventures, is attempting to purchase her property. They're also trying to purchase a vacant property Ken and his family own, along with a couple of others. I'm trying to figure out why the body was in Elvira's building. I'm still leaning toward Elvira's ex somehow being involved."

"Elvira's ex?" Sam smiled. "Poor guy."

"They have a daughter together, Zulilly, who showed up on Dernice's doorstep a few days ago, insisting her mother wants her here."

"Maybe you should do a little more digging around in the ex's background if that's your plan."

"It is."

Sam wished her luck and warned her to be careful before heading out.

Carlita set Mercedes' cell phone on the counter and wandered to the balcony doors. Dernice's back door was open, and the police car was still in the parking lot. It had been there for hours now.

Grayvie, who had followed her out, caught sight of a bluebird and let out a throaty growl, his tail thumping against the deck boards. He began making another noise as a second bird joined the first.

"You talking to the birdies, trying to convince them to come closer?" Carlita patted his head and returned inside, leaving the door open for him.

Deciding Ken Gibbons was still on her radar and that he needed a little more research, she switched her computer on and began digging into Sunrise Bar and Grill's history.

There were several stories about Gibbons receiving a hometown hero's welcome and a small quote from him about taking over the family business. The story was almost two years old.

She scrolled the screen and found another story, this one only a few weeks old about the family business experiencing financial woes. Carlita clicked on the link and discovered that the IRS was investigating them for tax evasion.

Carlita's head began to spin. Putting the pieces together, Gibbons had returned from active duty and discovered his family was in trouble with the IRS. What if Gibbons planned to use the sale of the property to pay off the family's debt, but there was a holdout – Elvira?

Hey! There was a commotion coming from the alleyway. Carlita scrambled out of the chair and dashed to the balcony door. She watched as a Savannah police officer escorted a handcuffed Dernice to the other end of the alley.

Chapter 24

Carlita snatched Grayvie up and darted back inside the apartment. She set the cat on the floor and ran out the door, not slowing until she reached the alley.

It was too late. The police car, with Dernice inside, was gone.

Elvira's back door was ajar. "Hello?" Carlita hollered as she took a tentative step inside. She called out again and could hear someone talking.

Carlita hurried through the apartment to the office where she found Zulilly pacing in front of the picture window, talking on her cell phone. She took one look at Carlita and turned her back.

"...with the evidence. Listen. I have company. I have to go." Zulilly abruptly ended the call. "Hello."

"Hello, Zulilly." Carlita got right to the point. "I watched the police drive off with your aunt in the back of a patrol car. What's going on?"

"The investigators have evidence linking Aunt D to the Tybee woman's death."

"What kind of evidence?"

"They found a rope and a note with the woman's name and address inside her work van." Zulilly's expression grew dark. "I suspected her all along. Aunt D was jealous of my mother."

"Why would she kill Kim Turbell? What does that have to do with Dernice being jealous of your mother?"

"It's obvious. To pin it on my mother. Her body was found in Mom's building. You know what I think?" Zulilly didn't wait for a reply. "Mom felt sorry for Aunt Dernice after she was released from prison and couldn't find a job, so she invited her to come to Savannah and help her with the businesses."

Zulilly proceeded to tell Carlita that after her mother left town, Dernice began concocting a plan. "My aunt knew my mom would be a suspect in the woman's murder. With Mom out of the picture, she could take over."

"I don't know if I buy that. Have you talked to your mother and told her what happened?"

"Not yet. I was getting ready to call her."

Carlita assumed Zulilly had been talking to Elvira, but apparently, she was already telling someone else. She had a sneaking suspicion that person was Zulilly's father.

It was possible Zulilly was correct. She knew the family dynamics and personalities better than Carlita. She remembered the other day when Dernice and she visited Coastal's sales office. After they left the building, Dernice went back inside and talked to the woman. What if she told Turbell she would meet her at the property later and then murdered her?

She dismissed the thought. The woman could have easily told co-workers or others she was meeting Dernice. Unless...Dernice told the woman she would be meeting Elvira.

Thoughts and theories tumbled around in Carlita's mind. There were too many suspects, too many possibilities. Somewhere in between was the truth.

Zulilly's cell phone rang, and she glanced at the screen. "I have to take this call. If you'll excuse me."

She strode to the front door and held it open, waiting for Carlita to exit.

Carlita could feel the woman's eyes on her as she walked past the front window. Something wasn't sitting right. Zulilly knew or was hiding something.

Carlita rounded the corner and collided with Luigi, who was heading in the opposite direction. He reached out to steady her. "Sorry. I didn't mean to plow you over."

"The police hauled Dernice off to jail. Zulilly seems to think she's responsible for the Tybee Island woman's death. I don't buy it."

"Dernice called me a little while ago. She said something about the heat was on, and she had a feeling she was gonna take the fall. I was on my way over to check on her." Luigi nodded in the direction of the building. "What about the daughter? Dernice thought she was up to no good."

"I was thinking the same thing. She's been talking to someone on her cell phone and was anxious for me to leave."

"So maybe it's her behind all of this," Luigi said.

"It could be. I don't trust her."

"If she's involved, she's gonna make a move."

"Make a move?"

"You know, tip her hand now that Dernice is out of the picture."

"You're right. We should keep an eye on her."

Luigi pulled his car keys from his pocket. "I owe Dernice one. I say we do a little surveillance on Elvira's dear daughter."

"A stakeout?"

"In your very own neighborhood."

"Let me go grab my purse." Carlita dashed up the stairs. She grabbed her purse and keys before joining Luigi, who was waiting for her at the other end of the alley. "Did she leave?"

"Not yet. Hop in." Luigi drove around the block and eased his car into a parking spot in front of Annie Dowton's real estate office, adjacent to their alley.

"Now what?" Carlita asked.

"We wait."

Carlita grew silent, keeping her eyes trained on the alley. Every few minutes, she glanced at her watch. "What if she doesn't leave?"

"She will."

Carlita texted Mercedes to let her know she was running an errand and then dialed Elvira's cell phone.

"Hey, Carlita. I was getting ready to give you a call. There's been a change of plans."

"Dernice is on her way to jail," Carlita blurted out.

"I heard. Zulilly thinks she's responsible for Turbell's death, that she was trying to set me up and take control of my businesses."

"There's something fishy going on over here."

"Yeah. It's looking like my sister is a conniving criminal and possibly even a killer."

"But what if it wasn't Dernice? What if the evidence the police found in her van had been planted?"

"By whom?"

Carlita wanted to say, "By your daughter," but knew that despite her strained relationship with

Zulilly, there was no way Elvira would suspect her daughter of being responsible. Instead, she decided to switch tactics. "When was the last time you talked to Zulilly?"

"Two minutes ago. She was getting ready to leave."

"But not before that?"

"No. Why?"

Carlita explained how she'd caught Zulilly on the phone, talking to someone. "It was right after Dernice's arrest, at least half an hour ago."

"I'm on my way. I'm waiting on my Uber," Elvira said. "I'll talk to her when I get home. What about other employees? Is anyone around?"

"No. Zulilly is the only one there."

"I'll handle it from here."

"But…" There was no chance to discuss it. Elvira had hung up on her.

Luigi draped his arm across the steering wheel. "She doesn't think her kid is involved."

"Not a chance." Carlita slid the phone in the pocket of her purse. She leaned her head back and closed her eyes. What if Zulilly was right, and Dernice had double-crossed her sister? After all, she had a criminal record and spent time in federal prison.

Was there jealousy between the sisters, perhaps even an underlying family feud? Did Dernice see an opportunity to take over while Elvira was out of the picture and dealing with her divorce?

There was still the issue of Ken Gibbons. He was in a tight spot with the IRS and needed money.

Mayor Clarence Puckett wasn't in the clear either. He was obviously deeply involved in Coastal Adventure's project and had a vested interest in ensuring the property owners sold, and the deal went through. The fact he had purchased the property through a trust was suspect. Why not list himself as the owner?

There was also Gremlin, Elvira's ex. He had both motive and opportunity, not to mention he had to have known Kim Turbell, at least in some capacity.

What if he had killed Kim Turbell and planted her body in Elvira's building knowing she would be a suspect? With Elvira in jail, Gremlin could ramp up the pressure for her to sell the property, not to mention potentially be in line to seize her assets and businesses if they were still legally married.

And now Carlita suspected Zulilly was more deeply involved than she previously thought. She had shown up on Elvira's doorstep for a reason.

"She's on the move." Luigi shifted the car into drive.

Carlita's head snapped up just in time to catch a glimpse of an EC Security Services' van as it turned the corner.

Zulilly didn't even glance in their direction as she stopped at the stop sign and continued through the intersection.

Luigi eased his vehicle onto the street keeping a safe distance between them.

Zulilly made several turns before backtracking at one point.

Carlita slid down in the seat as Zulilly did an illegal U-turn in the middle of the street. She passed by them, going in the opposite direction. "What is she doing?"

"We might be too close, and she suspects someone is tailin' her." Luigi followed suit and did a U-turn. "She's going faster."

They ran a light to keep up.

Zulilly slowed. Luigi slowed. "She's not onto us. I think she's lost."

They crossed over a set of railroad tracks, entering an area of town Carlita had only been in once.

The security services van pulled into a parking lot. Luigi steered his car onto the side of the street, a safe distance from the building.

They watched as Zulilly exited the van. She cast an anxious glance around and then hurried toward the building.

Carlita watched as she tried the door. "She's trying to get in," she whispered.

Zulilly pulled her cell phone from her back pocket.

"She's meeting someone." Carlita craned her neck. "What is this place?" She had no more finished asking the question when she spied a sign above the entrance. "I think we're close to cracking the case."

Chapter 25

Chirp. Carlita jumped at the sound of her cell phone. "It's Elvira. Hello?"

"Where are you?" Elvira asked. "I'm home. No one is around."

"Luigi and I followed Zulilly." Carlita rattled off the address.

"It's a business?"

"Yes, it is. Coastal Adventures."

"I...I. Are you sure? I had no idea they had an office in Savannah."

"Well, they do, and Zulilly is standing outside. It looks like she's waiting for someone."

There was heavy breathing on the other end of the line, and Carlita guessed Elvira was on the move. "I'm on my way. Don't go in. Wait for me. I'll be there in ten minutes, tops."

Carlita promised they would wait and then ended the call. "Should we call the cops?"

"And tell them what? We suspect Elvira's ex and possibly even her daughter killed someone?" Luigi asked. "We have no proof."

Despite the seriousness of the situation, Carlita smiled. "You sound like a cop. You sure you're not a former cop?"

"Would you believe me if I told you I went through the whole police academy thing and then changed my mind?"

"Yes...actually, no. No, I'm not surprised. Why..." her voice trailed off.

"Dirty cops. One of my best friends was gunned down by a dirty cop. It left a bad taste in my mouth."

"I'm sure it did. Not all cops are bad."

A four-door car passed by them and turned into the parking lot. The car parked next to Zulilly's security services' van. A thin man with curly gray hair exited the vehicle and met her at the door. They disappeared inside.

"Where is Elvira?" Carlita's armpits grew damp as she glanced behind her. "She better hurry up if she wants to be the one to confront her ex."

"Here she comes." A van sped past them.

Carlita could see Elvira behind the wheel, a grim expression on her face. She must've realized she went too far. The van circled back around before pulling in behind Luigi's vehicle.

Carlita exited the vehicle and joined her on the sidewalk. "You took long enough."

"I made it as fast as I could. Are they inside?"

"Yes." Carlita pointed to the car parked next to the security services van and described the man who was driving it.

"That's him…my ex."

Luigi made his way around the front.

Elvira gave him the once over. "I remember you."

"Elvira Cobb," Luigi said. "Glad you could make it to the party."

"Yeah, well, I'm here, and I don't need your help. I don't need a former mobster working for me. I have enough troubles."

"Elvira," Carlita chided. "I don't think you're in any position to judge. Besides, Dernice hired him."

"Look where she's at. She's in jail."

"Because of you."

"I'll cut you a check and bring it over later, after I get to the bottom of what's going on in there," Elvira said.

"You didn't hire me. You can't fire me."

"What do you mean?" Elvira's face turned bright red. "I can fire you, and I just did. You're fired."

"Nope." Luigi shook his head. "You're not my boss."

"I...I'm the owner," Elvira sputtered. "You're fired if I say you're fired."

Luigi threw her words back in her face.

She clenched her fists and took a menacing step toward him.

Luigi, cool as a cucumber, grinned, as if daring her to hit him, or perhaps he was simply amused by her reaction.

Carlita stepped between them. "We have bigger problems right now. We might need Luigi's muscle."

She could see Elvira considering her reasoning and relaxed her stance. "Fine. You can stay until I get to the bottom of what's going on. I have a gun in my glovebox."

Luigi patted his pocket. "I got it covered."

"Let's go." Carlita made a move toward the building.

Elvira hurried ahead of her. "I'll go in first."

Luigi brought up the rear, giving the vehicles the once over as they walked past. "Hang on."

"What is it?" Carlita asked.

"Check out the car," Luigi said.

Carlita studied the man's car. "What about it?"

"Over here." Luigi made his way to the passenger side and pointed to the missing mirror. "The mirror is missing. I shot it out the other day when the driver forced Dernice's van off the road."

Chapter 26

Carlita's breath caught in her throat. "You're right. This looks like the vehicle we saw. Elvira's ex, Gremlin, is behind all of this."

Luigi unzipped his jacket pocket. "This might get ugly."

"We have the element of surprise." Carlita tried to sound confident but knew they could very well be walking into a bad situation. She started to tell them she thought it was time to alert the authorities. It was too late. Elvira had already entered the building.

Luigi followed close behind while Carlita reluctantly brought up the rear.

Zulilly was the first to notice them. Her jaw dropped. "Mom? What are you doing here?"

"I'm here to talk to your father."

"I...I thought you were gonna be gone a while longer."

"Change of plans. When I found out the police picked Dernice up, I knew I needed to come home to see what was going on."

"I already told you. The police searched Dernice's van. They found evidence linking her to Kim Turbell's death and arrested her."

Elvira took a step forward, her attention focused on her ex. "Are you behind all of this, Gremlin?"

"I don't know what you're talking about."

"You knew Kim Turbell. She was an employee of a company of which you're part owner."

"It doesn't make me a killer. Besides, she was found in your building. Maybe you killed her."

"I barely even knew her. I was in another state when she was murdered. You know what I think? I think you had something to do with her death."

Elvira moved in for the kill. "Who shot out your passenger side mirror, Gremlin?"

"Dad didn't kill her." Zulilly straightened her shoulders and shot her mother a defiant look. "If you had sold the property like Dad asked you to, then none of this would've happened."

"How do you know?" Elvira asked her daughter. "How do you know your father isn't responsible?"

"Aunt D killed the woman," Zulilly insisted.

Elvira's voice softened. "I don't think she did. I think your father did it. In fact, I have a piece of evidence I believe the authorities will be very interested in taking a look at."

There was a look of fear in Zulilly's eyes. The fear disappeared, and her eyes flashed with anger. "This is all your fault. You were greedy and selfish. The only thing you were worried about was Dad not getting his hands on your businesses. But all you had to do was sell the property, and no one would've been hurt."

"Someone has been hurt. A woman is dead, and your aunt is at the police station."

The man with the mop of curly gray hair, placed a light hand on Zulilly's arm. "It's okay. I can handle this."

"Yes. Let your father handle this," Elvira mocked as she slowly crossed the room. "Let's talk."

"About what?"

"About the death of your employee, Kim Turbell."

"You're barking up the wrong tree. Your sister, a convicted felon, has been picked up."

"She didn't do it, and you know it. Zulilly as much as admitted you were behind this."

"I...you're twisting my words around," Zulilly's face crumpled, and Carlita almost felt sorry for the woman who looked like she was going to burst into tears.

"What were you doing, Grem?" Elvira asked in a soft voice. "You never were happy with just one woman. Were you having a fling with a married woman? Did you talk her into leaving her husband or boyfriend...the fling went south and, you did her in?"

"You're crazy...even crazier than before," he blustered.

"Am I? This is all beginning to make sense. You want the Tybee Island project to move forward. Unfortunately, your ex is standing in your way. As luck would have it, Zu offers to come down here to Savannah to help me, but she ends up helping you instead. You talk her into tracking my moves and Dernice's moves. I'm temporarily out of the picture, so you go after Dernice. Maybe my sister was figuring it out too."

"I'm calling the cops." Gremlin reached for his cell phone.

"Go ahead and call them. I'm sure they'll be interested in discovering the truth about what has been going on, maybe even dig a little deeper into your relationship with Kim Turbell."

339

"You've gone too far." Gremlin made a move for his desk. Luigi, despite his size, moved fast. He charged the man, knocking him off balance and sending him flying across the room.

Meanwhile, Elvira darted to the desk. She reached inside and pulled out a gun. "I think he was going for this."

Carlita, stunned by the turn of events, quickly recovered. She fumbled inside her purse for her cell phone and dialed 911. "Yes. This is Carlita Garlucci. We need the police at twenty-nine Magnolia Street as soon as possible."

She wasn't sure how Luigi managed to do it, but by the time she hung up, he had pinned Gremlin against the wall. "He ain't goin' anywhere."

It didn't take long for the police to arrive. All of them began talking at once with Elvira pointing fingers at Gremlin while Gremlin and Zulilly blamed Elvira.

The officers escorted Elvira, Luigi and Carlita outdoors. Gremlin and Zulilly remained inside while the police began searching.

A short time later, the officers led Gremlin and his daughter outside. "We'll let you inside after we finish searching the rest of the premises."

Gremlin's face grew deathly pale as he watched them through the window. "They don't have a search warrant. I want my attorney."

The officer, who was standing next to him, ignored the comment.

While Gremlin anxiously watched them search, Zulilly slumped against the wall and began muttering under her breath.

It seemed like forever before the officers finished and joined them. One was holding a manilla file folder. He reached inside the file folder and pulled out a greeting card. "Does this look familiar?"

Gremlin's face grew even paler as he stared at the card. He opened his mouth and then closed it

"This is a card addressed to you from 'Kim.'"

"Dreaming of our forever." The officer flipped the card open. "Wishing each moment was spent with you. It's signed, I love you forever, Kim."

Gremlin's eyes grew wide. "I...you have it all wrong. That's not from Kim Turbell. It's from another Kim."

"Kim who?" the officer asked.

"I want my lawyer," Gremlin finally said.

"You're under arrest for the death of Kim Turbell." The officer handed the envelope to his partner and began reading Gremlin his rights.

Zulilly sprang to her feet. "No. No! He didn't do it. I did it."

Gremlin grunted loudly, watching in horror as his daughter tried to tackle the officer.

The other officers sprang into action and quickly subdued her.

"Zu," Gremlin said. "Stop with the crazy talk. Neither of us killed Kim Turbell. Your mother or aunt are responsible."

Zulilly fought to break free. She flung herself to the side, so that she faced Elvira. Her eyes were dripping with hatred. "This is your fault," she spat out. "Yours and that stupid witch, Kim. She hated me. She tried to keep me from Dad. You don't deserve your businesses. Dad and I do."

"What are you saying?" Elvira whispered.

"You abandoned Dad and me years ago. You bought that property to spite him. If you had stayed out of it, none of this would've happened."

"Kim," Gremlin interrupted. "You killed Kim?"

Zulilly turned to her dad, her eyes half-crazed. "She didn't deserve you, so I lured her to Mom's place. She never even saw me until it was too late."

Zulilly calmly stated how she confronted Turbell at the real estate office where Turbell taunted her, claiming Gremlin would choose her over his daughter. "She was an evil woman. I did you a favor."

Shocked, Carlita struggled to put the pieces together. "The car. You tried to run your aunt, Luigi and me off the road."

"And I would've taken you out if not for this goon." Zulilly curled her lip and glared at Luigi.

"You borrowed my car and ran your aunt off the road?" Gremlin asked. "I thought you backed into a mailbox."

Carlita could see Gremlin was slowly realizing his daughter was not who he thought she was. "Don't say anything else, Zu. I'll get you a good lawyer."

The police finished reading the woman her rights and placed her in the back of the patrol car. As they drove off, Zulilly glared at them through the back window. Her lips were moving, and she stared her mother down.

"I…I'm sorry, Elvira. I had no idea," Gremlin said. "I had no idea Zulilly killed Kim. I thought you did it."

"And I thought *you* did it." Elvira's shoulder's sagged, and Carlita thought she was going to burst into tears. "My daughter has been taken from me all over again." She gave her ex a defeated look and began shuffling away.

Gremlin wasn't off the hook, either. The police escorted him to the back of another vehicle and placed him inside.

Carlita caught up with Elvira by her van. "I'm sorry, Elvira."

"I had no idea." Elvira clutched her gut, a pained expression on her face. "I feel like I lost my daughter all over again."

Concerned over Elvira's state of mind, Carlita drove them home with Luigi following behind in his car. When they reached the apartment, Carlita offered to run down to the police station to check on Dernice.

A subdued Elvira thanked her and trudged into her apartment. Luigi offered to tag along and climbed into the passenger seat. "That's one messed up family."

"It is." Carlita consulted the rearview mirror before backing out of the parking lot. "I thought it was Gremlin."

"Me too."

At the precinct, Carlita and Luigi waited for nearly an hour before Detective Wilson joined them in the front lobby. "Mrs. Garlucci."

"Hello, Detective Wilson. We're here to see if Dernice Cobb will be released soon."

"As a matter of fact, she'll be ready to go shortly."

Dernice emerged. She spotted Carlita and Luigi and hurried over. "The detective told me you were out here waiting. That was a fun time."

"Thank you for your cooperation in our investigation, Ms. Cobb." The detective smiled. "You're free to leave."

"What happened?" Dernice followed Carlita and Luigi out of the building. "I was in for my fifth round of interrogations when someone came in and said I was free to go."

"Because they have Kim Turbell's killer in custody."

"Seriously?" Dernice abruptly stopped. "Do you know who it is?"

"Zulilly. Your niece hated the woman. She lured her to Elvira's property and killed her."

"That's heavy. What about Gremlin?"

"They brought him in too. He was much more involved with Kim Turbell than any of us knew. If what Zulilly says is true and she murdered Kim Turbell, I'm sure he'll eventually be cleared." Carlita continued. "Your sister is home and taking it hard. She needs you right now."

347

"Poor Elvira. I'm sure she's devastated."

Carlita had barely finished parking the car when Dernice bolted from the vehicle. She was already inside the apartment by the time Carlita and Luigi walked past.

Mercedes heard her mother return home and wandered out of her room, still wearing her pajamas. "What happened to you?"

"What hasn't happened? Dernice was picked up for questioning. Elvira is back. Her daughter is responsible for Kim Turbell's death."

"Zulilly?"

"Yep."

"And I missed all of that?"

"Yes, you missed all of that."

*****

Two days passed before Elvira stopped by to tell Carlita that Zulilly had been admitted to the prison's mental health ward. "Zulilly still believes she did her father a favor by killing the woman."

"What about you and Gremlin? Are you speaking to each other?"

"We are. He's devastated. I'm devastated. It's a mess."

"I've been wondering about something," Carlita said. "Dernice was convinced someone was messing around your place right before Turbell was killed."

"It was Gremlin. He was sneaking around, trying to find out where I went. My surveillance cameras are hunks of junk. I'm replacing every single one. He found out Zu was coming to Savannah and convinced her to keep an eye on Dernice and me. Zu tracked Kim down, they got into a huge argument about Gremlin and that's when Zu lured her to my property." Elvira placed her hands on her hips. "Gremlin thought Luigi was my boyfriend. Can you believe it?"

"Yeah. I can see you two as a couple," Carlita joked.

"That's not funny," Elvira said. "Thanksgiving is right around the corner. You gonna have a big shindig again this year?"

"I am. I'm hosting a Thanksgiving Day dinner at the restaurant at six o'clock for family and friends."

"Dernice and I will be there."

Carlita sighed. She hadn't invited Elvira. In fact, she'd made a point not to, deciding to save herself some unneeded aggravation and potential drama. "You just invited yourself."

"But I was invited last year. You weren't planning on inviting me?" Elvira's expression was incredulous.

"I figured I didn't need the extra aggravation."

"Are you trying to tell me I'm aggravating?" Elvira's eyebrows furrowed. "We're like family...not *the* family, but you know. We've been through a lot together."

"I can't argue the point."

"Gremlin is in rough shape. Do you mind if I invite him too?"

"Are you divorced?" Carlita answered the question with one of her own.

"Finally." Elvira swiped her palms together. "I spent a small fortune in lawyers' fees, but our divorce is final. Maybe we can repair our relationship now that we're officially exes and can commiserate over our woes. So, we'll see you at six?"

Carlita closed her eyes. "Fine. Yes. I'll see you at six Thursday."

"Great. I'll bring a big pot of natto."

"I can hardly wait."

Chapter 27

The next few days flew by as Carlita geared up for her Thanksgiving Day feast. Not only was she serving two large turkeys and her version of her mother-in-law's eggplant parmesan, but she also planned to make a family favorite – homemade Italian stuffing. There would also be candied yams, smashed potatoes, corn on the cob, sweet butter rolls, pumpkin pie and an array of decadent desserts.

When the big day arrived, Carlita spent part of it working in the restaurant. It was the first big holiday for Ravello's, and she wasn't sure what to expect. The crowds were steady, but not overwhelming.

After the last guest left and they closed for the day, she helped the kitchen staff clean up.

Her children arrived a short time later – Tony, Shelby and Mercedes, along with her granddaughter, Violet. Since Carlita had prepped most of the food early that morning and the turkeys were already roasting, it didn't take long for them to finish preparing the feast.

Sam and Cool Bones were the first to arrive. The men sprang into action and began sliding the tables together. Autumn, her brother Steve, and his girlfriend, Paisley, were next. Luigi was right behind them. Tori Montgomery, Byron, Annie Dowton and Reese followed him in.

Elvira, along with her sister, wandered into the kitchen, each of them carrying a large bowl.

"Do you want us to put our dishes on the table?" Elvira asked.

Carlita wrinkled her nose. "Did you bring your natto?"

"Yes." Elvira cradled the dish. "And don't turn your nose up. This is not only delicious and nutritious, but it's also good for your digestive system."

"I'm sure someone will try it," Carlita said diplomatically. "Put it anywhere on the table where you can find an empty spot."

"I brought my homemade cabbage and noodles," Dernice said.

"Now *that* I will most definitely have to try." Carlita juggled the baskets of fresh dinner rolls and rushed through the kitchen doors, nearly colliding with Pete, who was the last to arrive and bearing a bouquet of fall flowers.

"Let me help." He grabbed one of the baskets and followed Carlita to the table.

"Thank you." Carlita placed the rolls on the table and eyed the flowers. "Flowers again? You're going to spoil me."

"You're onto my secret plan." Pete sneaked in a quick kiss. "You've got quite a crowd."

"I do. Isn't it wonderful?"

Annie Dowton cornered Pete to discuss the sale of his ranch. Carlita's other guests gathered in small groups, chatting while Tony and Shelby made their rounds greeting everyone and offering them beverages.

Satisfied everything was ready to go, Carlita slipped back into the dining room and stood watching from the doorway. Her throat clogged as she gazed around the room at her family and friends.

A feeling of melancholy filled her as she thought about her husband, Vinnie, and her other children and grandchildren who weren't there.

Pete caught her eye and wandered over. He leaned in and squeezed her hand. "Everything looks lovely, lass. You outdid yourself."

"Thanks. I...it was a labor of love. I'm so glad everyone could make it." Her eyes drifted to Elvira, who was talking with Cool Bones. "Even Elvira, I suppose."

"She considers you family."

"She said as much."

"I was shocked to hear her daughter killed the Tybee Island woman."

"I was too. I'm still shaking my head over that one."

"Luigi told me he likes his job working for EC Security Services, that they're keeping him on."

"Yes. Much to Elvira's dismay. For some reason, the two of them are like oil and water, constantly butting heads."

"Perhaps they're too much alike," Pete guessed.

"Could be. They're both bullheaded and impulsive."

"It sounds like a match made in heaven."

"Doesn't it?"

Carlita enlisted the help of her children, who followed her into the kitchen. They each grabbed a dish or tray of food and carried them into the dining room.

Byron joined them. "Let me help."

"Then, you get the honor of carrying the turkeys." Violet, who began following Byron around from the moment he arrived, tagged along behind him.

Tray after tray of food was carried to the long L-shaped dinner table until there wasn't an empty spot left.

Carlita motioned to Pete. "I need to get everyone's attention."

"Can I do the honors?" Pete asked.

"Yes. Of course."

Pete lifted a glass and lightly tapped the side with a fork. "Attention, everyone."

The room grew quiet.

"Thank you to the Garlucci family for inviting us to this Thanksgiving Day celebration. We all have so much to be thankful for – for God's blessing and to live in this beautiful City of Savannah."

"We most certainly do," Carlita's eyes burned as she blinked back sudden tears.

Tony lifted his goblet of water. "Here's to family and friends."

Carlita lifted her glass. "To family and friends," she echoed. "Now, let's eat."

The end.

If you enjoyed reading "Exes and Woes in Savannah," would you please take a moment to leave a review? It would mean so much. Thank you! –Hope Callaghan

The Series Continues... Book 15 in the "Made in Savannah" Series Coming Soon!

Books in This Series

Made in Savannah Cozy Mystery Series

A mother and daughter try to escape their family's NY mob ties by making a fresh start in Savannah, GA but they soon realize you can run but you can't hide from the past.

Get New Releases & More

Get New Releases, Giveaways & Discounted eBooks When YouSubscribe To My Free Cozy Mysteries Newsletter!

hopecallaghan.com/newsletter

Meet Author Hope Callaghan

Hope loves to connect with her readers! Connect with her today!

Never miss another book deal! Text the word Books to 33222

Visit **hopecallaghan.com/newsletter** for special offers, free books,
and soon-to-be-released books!

Hope Callaghan is an American author who loves to write clean fiction books, especially Christian Mystery and Cozy Mystery books. She has written more than 70 mystery books (and counting) in six series.

In March 2017, Hope won a Mom's Choice Award for her book, "Key to Savannah," Book 1 in the Made in Savannah Cozy Mystery Series.

Born and raised in a small town in West Michigan, she now lives in Florida with her husband. She is the proud mother of 3 wonderful children.

When she's not doing the thing she loves best - writing books - she enjoys cooking, traveling and reading books.

Eggplant Parmesan Recipe

(Shared by Barbara Tooley)

Ingredients:

3 eggplants, peeled and thinly sliced

2 eggs, beaten

4 cups Italian seasoned breadcrumbs

6 cups spaghetti sauce, divided

1 - 16-ounce package mozzarella cheese, shredded and divided

½ cup grated Parmesan cheese, divided

½ teaspoon dried basil

Directions:

-Preheat oven to 350 degrees F (175 degrees C).

-Dip eggplant slices in egg, then in breadcrumbs. Place in a single layer on a baking sheet. Bake in preheated oven for 5 minutes on each side.

-In a 9x13 inch baking dish spread spaghetti sauce to cover the bottom.

-Place a layer of eggplant slices in the sauce.

-Sprinkle with mozzarella and Parmesan cheeses.

-Repeat with remaining ingredients, ending with the cheeses.

-Sprinkle basil on top.

-Bake in preheated oven for 35 minutes, or until golden brown.

Hot Milk Sponge Cake Recipe

(Shared by Rita McDonnell)

Ingredients:

4 eggs

2 cups sugar

2 cups flour

2 teaspoons baking powder

2 teaspoons vanilla

1 cup hot whole milk

Directions:

- Preheat oven to 350 degrees.

- Blend flour and baking powder in medium size mixing bowl. Set aside.

- Place eggs in separate (larger) bowl.

- Using mixer, beat eggs.

- After eggs are beaten, add sugar and continue beating until blended.

- Gradually add dry mixture to eggs and sugar while

continuing to beat.

- Add vanilla. Blend thoroughly.

- Add hot milk to mixture last and beat one final time.

- After all of the ingredients are blended, pour into ungreased tube pan.

- Bake for about one hour.

*Serve with fruit.

67520976R00220